Love You

Hate You

Miss You

Also by Elizabeth Scott:

STEALING HEAVEN

Love You

Hate You

Miss You

❧

ELIZABETH SCOTT

HARPERTEEN

An Imprint of HarperCollins*Publishers*

HarperTeen is an imprint of HarperCollins Publishers.

Library of Congress Cataloging-in-Publication Data

Scott, Elizabeth, date.

Love you hate you miss you / Elizabeth Scott. — 1st ed.

p.   cm.

Summary: After coming out of alcohol rehabilitation, sixteen-
year-old Amy sorts out conflicting emotions about her best friend
Julia's death in a car accident for which she feels responsible.

ISBN 978-0-06-112283-5 (trade bdg.)

ISBN 978-0-06-112284-2 (lib. bdg.)

[1. Guilt—Fiction. 2. Death—Fiction. 3. Self-perception—
Fiction. 4. Alcoholism—Fiction. 5. Schools—Fiction. 6. Best
friends—Fiction. 7. Friendship—Fiction.] I. Title.

PZ7.S4195Lo 2009   2008031420

[Fic]—dc22   CIP

                                                              AC

Typography by Ray Shappell

09 10 11 12 13 LP/RRDB 10 9 8 7 6 5 4 3 2 1

❖

First Edition

ACKNOWLEDGMENTS

Thanks to Tara Weikum for believing in me and this book—and for her incredible heart and talent.

Thanks also to Katharine Beutner, Clara Jaeckel, Shana Jones, Jess Lewis-Turner, Amy Pascale, Donna Randa-Gomez, Nephele Tempest, and Janel Winter for their insightful comments and kindness.

Extra special thanks to Robin Rue for all her support.

This book is absolutely, positively, 110% for Jessica Brearton, who deserves at least a parade in her honor.

Jess, you believed in me when I'd lost my way, and wouldn't let me give up on writing. Thank you not just for the encouragement to finish this, but for your friendship—and for simply being you.

Love You

Hate You

Miss You

75 days

Dear Julia,

Get this, I'm supposed to be starting a journal about "my journey." Please. I can see it now:

> *Dear Diary,*
> *As I'm set adrift on this crazy sea called "life," I like to think of an inspirational poem I heard not long ago, one that made me weep because of its beauty. Today, I truly believe each day is a precious gift. . . .*

I don't think so.

Anyway, while Dr. Marks (mustache like you wouldn't believe, long and shaggy and made even worse by the fact that he's always got crumbs in it) babbles on about how we need a place to share our "experiences," I'm writing to you.

I don't want you to think everything here has been so useless. I mean, Pinewood is a "teen treatment center," so there's, you know, the unpleasantness of just being here, but it hasn't all sucked. It's going to follow me around forever, though. "Was in rehab." Just like all the other " " I carry now.

You know, I always thought I told you everything, but there are some things I should have said and never did. I should have told you about the time I lost your new sunglasses. I know you really liked them. I should have apologized every time I puked on your shoes and especially the time I ruined your brand-new skirt, the one with the beading. I should have apologized for a lot of stuff.

I'm sorry. I'm sorry for everything.

It's been seventy-four days since I had a drink. I miss it. I miss the way it made me feel, how I didn't seem so tall and stupid, how everything went soft around the edges. I've even been dreaming about it. I'm told this is normal, though. I'm told I can still leave. I'm "better," you see, and the world is waiting.

Dr. Marks just asked if I'm okay. He's such a freak. I don't know how he ended up in charge of group therapy. You should hear how he talks, you really should. He can't say my name like a normal person. Amy. How hard is that to say? But Dr. Marks always calls me

Amyyyyyyyyyyyyyyyyyyyyy, like y is a letter he doesn't get to use often enough.

I think about you all the time. I tell everyone in group I picture you swooping in to check up on everything, an angel with kick-ass wings, but I actually wonder if you're cold or if you get to wear your purple sweater all the time because it's your favorite and your mom isn't around to tell you it's too low-cut.

Right now, I wonder if you're singing one of those stupid love songs you love so much and if they still make you smile. I wonder if you miss driving across the Millertown bridge while we take turns eating ice cream. You were always able to smuggle a pint out of the grocery store. If I close my eyes I can see you laughing, spoon in hand. I haven't eaten ice cream in months.

I've cried a lot in Pinewood, and always about you. I know that must seem strange, especially since you know that before I didn't cry at all. I wanted to, though—you know that too, right? But I couldn't. I knew if I did I'd never stop.

I suppose I should be happy about getting out of here tomorrow. I guess I am, but the thing is, I keep thinking about who I want to see when I get home and . . . there's no one. You won't be there.

I miss you, J.

ONE

RELEASE DAY CAME, as promised, and I got my stuff together in the morning. I didn't have a roommate, and I didn't really talk to anyone, so I was ready to go pretty quick. (Group therapy was enough conversation for me.)

And that was it. Good-bye Pinewood, thanks for all the crap food and "sharing sessions." Couldn't say I was going to miss any of it.

Laurie, my shrink, came and walked down with me.

"What are you thinking about?" I don't think Laurie knows how to not ask questions. Must be the first thing they teach in shrink school. Also seems to be the only thing.

"Nothing."

"It's okay to be scared," she said, and I did that thing with my eyebrows Julia's mom always called snotty.

4

Laurie didn't seem to notice. She just said, "Everyone gets scared," like it was some big profound statement.

"Wow, thanks," I said.

"Your parents are waiting, Amy," she said. "They're right out there and they're excited about taking you home."

The sick thing is, I wanted to believe her. I wanted to believe that Mom and Dad were waiting and actually wanted to see me. I'd thought that part of me, the part that wanted me and Mom and Dad to be a family and not how we actually are, which is the two of them and then me, was gone. I thought I'd killed it, smashed it into pieces so small they'd never fit together again. I guess I was wrong.

"Fine," I said, and went to meet them.

They were there in the waiting room, sitting curled up in each other's arms on one of the sofas. My first day at Pinewood, my arms were raw from where I'd dug my fingers in to make sure I was alive, and they'd sat on that same sofa the exact same way.

I'd sat across from them and watched them clutch each other's hands like they'd be lost if they let go. They'd given me a weird almost hug when I left, the two of them still clutching each other and trying to squeeze me in. That was a lot of fun.

Today they were clutching hands again, but they actually let go of each other and got up and hugged me. Separately. That's when I realized today was going to be weird. As in seriously weird.

I'm taller than both of them now. I can't believe it. I knew I was taller than Mom but didn't realize I'm taller than Dad. I guess maybe I grew some while I was here. It figures. Sixteen, about six feet tall, and just out of a "treatment center." I'm such a winner.

On the drive home, Mom and Dad told me about my "new" room. My bedroom up in the attic is gone. They moved all my stuff down into the guest room on the second floor, and now it's my bedroom. I can't believe my parents want me sleeping near them. Weird. But then I suppose it fits in with today.

Because after telling me about my new room, my parents had other things to say. They told me there wouldn't be a lock on my door anymore. They told me that even though I'm now old enough to get my license, there's no way I was going to. They also told me I would have to keep seeing Laurie every week.

I said "Fine" to everything. I think they expected arguing or something because they kept looking at me, Dad in the rearview mirror, Mom in the little one you're supposed to use to check your makeup.

When we got here the weirdness was complete, because the house . . . it's still the same, but yet it isn't. For one thing, it's blue now. Apparently, Mom had it painted again. It's better than the yellow it was before but not by much. I don't know how an art professor can be so clueless when it comes to this stuff. I mean, she can paint and teach other people how to do it, but she can't figure out that a blue house is a bad idea?

Mom and Dad might have been waiting for me to comment on the house. You never know with them. I didn't say anything. It's a new color, not a new house, not a new me and a new them, and Julia is still gone.

They helped me bring my stuff in, and then we all stood around looking at one another. I finally said, "I'm hungry," just so it wasn't so quiet. They, of course, both went to fix me something to eat. I know they don't do everything together, and I've even heard them argue once in a while, but most of the time it's like they're one person. Not Colin and Grace. Just ColinandGrace.

I can hear them now, laughing at a joke they'll never share with me. If Julia was here I never would have heard it because we'd be out having fun. I don't care about my room or a stupid lock or driving or even having to see Laurie. I don't care about any of it.

76 days

J,

It's me. I'm home, though it doesn't feel like it. Not without you.

I tossed the starter journal Dr. Marks gave me, which is just as well because it had little pine trees running along the bottom of every page. I suppose I should be happy it wasn't teddy bears.

After I tossed it and a bunch of other random crap Pinewood gave me, pamphlets and books and bullshit about feelings, I found my old chemistry notebook.

Remember chemistry?

Me neither. I know I passed because I wore a short skirt every time we had a test. Mr. Lansing was such a pervert. Neither of us took a single note all year. I flipped through the notebook when I pulled it out and it was blank page after blank page except for one.

Hey, you wrote me a note at the bottom of this page.

"Locker after class?"

Your handwriting is so much nicer than mine.

I just called your house. Your mother hung up as soon as I said hello.

TWO

78 DAYS TODAY, and Mom took me to the mall.

"A belated birthday present," she said.

I wasn't allowed to get gifts while I was in Pinewood. Laurie had asked me how I felt about that at least a hundred times, but what did I care? What kind of birthday was it without Julia there? In the end it was just another day of therapy and bad food punctuated with an awkward visit with Mom and Dad.

They sang "Happy Birthday" and asked me how my room was, then stood around looking nervous. It was a visit just like all their others, except for the song. Laurie had asked me about that too. She has a question for everything.

Mom and Dad were both going to take me to the mall, but last night at dinner we were talking (by which I mean

I just sat there and tried to think of things to say when they asked me stuff—until now, dinner was always a two-person show) and Dad suggested she and I go since Mom wasn't teaching today. He said he'd take me to get school supplies over the weekend.

Mom looked hurt (oh no, they weren't going to be doing everything together!) and Dad reached out and took her hand, giving her the "you're my whole world" look. I don't get how they can be so into each other. It's not normal. (Julia thought it was sweet, but then she was in love with the whole idea of love. In my book being that "in love" is, frankly, kind of creepy.)

Anyway, they were holding hands and finishing each other's sentences and Dad was starting to talk about trying to rearrange his schedule. I could feel myself fading, becoming invisible girl once again, but then Mom said, "You know, I think that's a great idea."

She almost sounded like she meant it. Almost.

We went, just the two of us, and I spent the first ten minutes waiting for her to shrivel up because Dad wasn't around. She seemed fine, though.

Me—well, that was different. The mall was bigger than I remembered, too full of crap and people. One of the first stores we passed was the one where me and Julia almost got busted for putting a skirt in my purse. I'd wanted to grab a plaid one, but she'd found one that was so much cooler. She had this gift of being able to find the most amazing clothes in any store. Two seconds and she'd have the perfect outfit, an outfit that no one else but her could wear.

Anyway, she picked the skirt, it was in my bag, and we almost exploded trying not to laugh on our way out of the store.

I couldn't breathe, thinking about that. How hard we tried not to laugh. How hard she did once we were back out in the mall again, her head thrown back and her eyes shining.

Julia always laughed so loudly, so happily.

I'm never going to hear her laugh again.

Everything started going fuzzy then, black around the edges.

"Mom," I said. "I have to sit down."

Mom took me to the food court, bought me a soda, and called Dad. I didn't bother listening to the conversation because no one needs to hear "I love you" forty-seven million times. You'd think they'd get sick of saying it to each other. I know they never will.

Mom wouldn't take me home when I finished my soda. I said, "But what about Dad?" and she said, "He's fine. Which store do you want to go to first?"

So we went shopping. What else could I do? We went into store after store, Mom looking, me standing there, trying to breathe. She kept showing me these little skirts and shirts, stuff like—stuff like Julia and me always wore.

She even said, "If I had your figure . . . ," and I stared at her until she said, "Oh, Amy, I understand. You and Julia probably came here, right?" and squeezed my hand.

I'd always wanted to do this kind of thing with her, go shopping, do mom-and-daughter stuff I should have stopped longing for in middle school. I never wanted it to be like this.

On the way home, Mom asked about birth control, the question too casual to be anything but practiced at least a hundred times. I told her there was nothing to tell.

She said, "I know there must be," so I told her I knew all about it and had been extra careful ever since I had to take a pregnancy test when I was fourteen. I shouldn't have done it, but I didn't want to talk about sex with Mom and I knew that would stop the conversation.

It did, and I thought about the day Julia told me she needed to buy a pregnancy test. She'd cried and then wiped her eyes and smiled at me. She'd said, "It'll be okay."

I should have said that to her. I should have said something. Done something. Anything. Instead I just sat there.

I thought about sitting in Julia's bathroom, holding her hand as we waited for the results. She spun around in circles after the little stick showed everything would be fine, turning and turning with a smile on her face. We went to a party that night, and she got so high she fell in a bathtub and split her lip open. I tried to clean her up and ended up smearing blood all over her shirt.

We both pretended she wasn't crying.

As Mom and I finished our drive home in silence, I thought about the mall again.

I'd seen Kevin there. Trailing Mom from one store to another and there he was, standing with his jerkass friends, hanging out. When he saw me, he glared, as if he's in so much pain. No matter how much he wishes Julia was here, I wish it more.

I pretended I didn't see him, and watched Mom flip through shirts I wouldn't let her buy me.

I pretended I didn't feel like my heart was breaking.

80 days

J,

Dad and I went to one of those huge office supply stores this afternoon. I now have more notebooks and pens than anyone could ever need. When I was shopping with Mom we couldn't really talk because I was constantly trying on things and telling her I didn't want them. (Plus I think she was mentally rehearsing for the sex conversation.) With Dad there was a lot more silence to fill because it's not like there's a lot to talk about when it comes to notebooks.

I did learn I'm going to be a junior—I guess my final grades from last year were better than you'd said they'd be. Also, on the first day of school, I have to go in with Mom so we can meet with a guidance counselor and talk about "my future."

I was looking at pens when Dad told me that, and I thought about the first day of school last year. We were at your locker, bitching about our schedules, and Kevin walked by and said, "Hi." You smiled at him. That was how you two began.

I'd been hoping I wouldn't be let back into school at all.

I picked up a package of pens and ignored Dad, who was still talking. I didn't want to remember past that, the first day of school last year and your smile, but I did. I remembered the party, remembered your devastated face. Remembered looping my arm through yours that night and saying, "Let's go, everything will be fine, school's finally over and summer's here. Screw Kevin and his freshman skank, you can do better and you will. It'll be okay. We just need to get out of here."

We walked out of the party, warm night air blowing over us, and didn't look back. I was proud of myself, you know. I really was.

"My future," and there's another " " for me to hate.

I told Dad we had to leave and sat in the car while he paid. We came home and I've been here, in my room, ever since.

And I—

I want a drink so bad. I just want that moment where all my worries melt into warmth. I want that moment where everything feels right, you know?

I don't deserve to have that feeling.

I still want it anyway.

THREE

I'M GOING BACK to school soon. Very soon, in fact. Tomorrow is the big day.

Tomorrow is too soon.

After I found out, after Dad told me, and after I wrote to Julia, I had to— I couldn't stand being in my own skin. I couldn't stand myself.

I went up to the attic. I looked around, sat on the floor, and then got up again. Mom and Dad found me there after a while, looking for something to drink.

They made an emergency therapy appointment for me right away. I hate that I've become a bunch of quotation marks. "In Recovery." "At Risk."

"Murderer."

Julia's mother screamed that at me in the emergency room the night Julia died. She screamed it and screamed it and then stopped, stared at me with her face drawn tighter than I'd ever seen it. She stared at me and then whispered it.

The screaming I hadn't even really heard—it's how Julia's mother always talks—but that whisper, that little cracked sound. *Murderer.* It hangs heavy around me. Inside me.

It is me.

Laurie didn't seem too surprised that I ended up coming to see her a couple of days before I'm supposed to. She said it was "good" I didn't drink, and it was still "good" even after I pointed out that I would have if I'd found something.

"But you didn't find anything, did you?" she said.

"I wanted to," I said, and then she clicked her pen twice and gave me one of her "I see something you don't" looks. I hate it when she does that. I hate her pen clicking too.

Mom drove me home after, and stayed with me because the university was closed for Labor Day. I went up to my room, and when she came to check on me she seemed surprised to find me lying on my bed, flipping through one of her art books.

I suppose given everything she and Dad were forced to realize once they had to face up to the fact that, "hey, we have a kid and she's really messed up," she expected to find me squatting on my bed cutting my hair with nail scissors or something.

I sort of wished I'd obliged her. Their whole trying-to-care thing is too strange.

Anyway, she did the "I care" thing, sat down next to me, and said, "I have a better book about that period. Would you like to see it?"

"No," I said. I was looking at the book because it was Julia's favorite, the one she always flipped through after she came over and smoked a joint out the attic window and then bitched at me for never doing it with her. Pot never made me mellow like it did her. It just made me hungry and tired.

"Well, would you like to go somewhere?"

"No," I said again, and she frowned and asked me if I wanted a cigarette.

I said, "What?"

"Well," she said. "Every time your father and I visited you at—at Pinewood, you always smelled like smoke. And I know that . . . I know giving up drinking has been hard, and I don't want you to think that your father and I don't understand that. So if you want, we could set up a little area outside, maybe near the edge of my flower garden, and you could—"

"I don't smoke," I said.

"Oh," she said, and then sat there looking at me.

I stared at the book. What did Julia see in the pictures? I wish I'd asked her. I thought about what she'd say if I had until Mom left.

I wanted Mom to say, "Why don't you smoke?"

I wanted to tell her I used to, that Julia and I started the summer her mom threatened to send Julia to stay with her aunt because she was being more paranoid than usual. (Just thinking about J's imitation of her mother's "Are you on DRUGS?" speech makes me smile.)

I wanted to tell Mom I stopped because the night I looked into Julia's unseeing eyes I had a cigarette in my hand, that despite everything it was still between my fingers, the red tip sparking faintly, just waiting for me to breathe it back to life. All around us, the air smelled like burned rubber and cracked metal, and my cigarette still glowed as the world ended.

I haven't smoked since. I learned to live with the sight and smell of them at Pinewood even though I went out of my way to avoid it, always making sure I washed my clothes if they started to smell, and lathering my hair until my fingers were numb and smelled of nothing but cheap shampoo. And the thought of having one, of breathing in and out and watching it burn—I could never do that again. Not now. Not ever.

82 days

J,

I'm sitting in the bathroom. The teachers' bathroom, even. You remember the signs, and how they'd glare if it looked like we might walk near it. It's not much nicer than our bathrooms though, which surprised me. You'd think all the glaring would at least protect something interesting.

I'm pretty sure as long as I don't move, as long as I stay right here, invisible—well, if I do that, I think my first day at school will be just fine.

Mrs. Griggles was the guidance counselor me and Mom had to see. She actually tried to look happy when we showed up. She ended up looking like someone had shoved a lemon in her mouth. Good old Giggles. (I wish you'd been there to call her that. I could never work up the nerve.) I thought she was going to explode when she saw the suggested class schedule Pinewood had put together for me. I kind of thought I might explode.

One of the things I had to do at Pinewood was take a bunch of tests. You know, in case I was "developmentally damaged" from drinking. I refused to see the results—what did they matter? The only thing I like is words, and English in Lawrenceville County schools is all about stomping the enjoyment of them out of you. School is a waste of time, and school without you wasn't something I wanted to think about, but apparently I'm not developmentally damaged at all. In fact, I may have started drinking because I "wasn't challenged enough in class." I bet you anything Laurie wrote that. Pen clicking idiot.

So anyway, instead of my normal schedule of study halls and low expectations, I'm taking honors English, honors U.S. history, honors physics, French, math analysis, and psychology. (I smell Laurie in that one too.) When Giggles was reading the list I tried to say, "No, I don't want this," but my throat had dried up, and when I glanced at my mother she looked like a stranger.

For a second, I forgot and looked around for you, because when I'm in Giggles's office it's always with you.

It was always with you. God, J. *Was.* You should have

been there, but you weren't. You never will be again. I had to get out of there then, so I asked to go to the bathroom.

I was actually going to leave, but halfway down the hall I realized where I was going. I'd automatically headed for it.

Your locker.

I saw it, J. Do you know what they've done to it? It's plastered with foil stars covered with glitter. On the stars are bad poems and little messages about you. People MISS YOU! and LOVE YOU!! and are THINKING OF YOU!!! I opened it—it was unlocked—and inside was the same thing. All your stuff was gone. The card Kevin got you for your six-month anniversary. The pictures of you and me. Your makeup bag. The plastic bag way in the back, the one you always kept filled with tiny liquor bottles for me and a couple of pills for you. The coat you never wore and the picture of you and your mom where you were both smiling for real that you kept hidden in the pocket. It was all gone, replaced by fake stars and fake words.

I wanted to tear it all down. You could have. You would have. You always knew what to do, what to say. You knew how to make anyone smile or shut the hell up. You dyed your hair purple with Kool-Aid for kicks and made snoring noises when Giggles lectured us about being late. Even drunk I could never do those things.

So now I'm here, at school, hiding out in the teachers' bathroom, and I don't know what to do. I can't leave, Julia. I'm just stuck here freaking out. If I close my eyes, will you come to me? You don't have to make everything all right. You don't have to do anything. I just want you here. Just for a second.

Please.

82 days

J,

Me again. Guess where I am?

History class. Excuse me, *honors* history. Mom found me in the teachers' bathroom. I wanted to ask how she had but couldn't. I don't know how to.

"You're a very smart girl, Amy," she said, and it was weird to be sitting locked in a toilet stall and hear that. It was weirder hearing Mom say it. "You have an opportunity for . . ." She trailed off then, which was good because I was afraid she was going to say something like "a new start" or "a second chance." I was afraid she'd say something I have no idea how to get and wouldn't be able to even if I did.

I was afraid she'd say something I don't deserve to hear.

This one girl keeps staring at me. She looks kind of familiar. She has very straight, very blond hair and is totally adorable in that way only girls like her can be. You'd imitate her, make me laugh and forget I'm a million feet tall and not adorable at all.

There are two guys looking at me too. I think maybe I made out with the first one once or something because he looked away when I stared back at him. He probably has a girlfriend, and she's probably in this class too. Great. The other one guy—I don't know. There's something about him, plus when I looked at him he just stared back at me. That's not what guys do when I look at them. They smile and look away or just look away. I don't get it.

That girl is *still* staring at me. This is going to be a very long day.

FOUR

I HADN'T MADE OUT with the guy who looked away. In fact, I hadn't done anything with him. The more I looked at him, the more I was sure I didn't even know him. I mean, I'd seen him around at a few parties, but that's how it is with parties. Or at least it's how it is with the ones around here. You see everyone at them eventually.

In English he sat down near me, smiled, and said, "Hey, I'm Mel."

"Hey," I said back, and noticed everyone—by which I mean the girls—was watching me. It was easy to figure out why. Mel would be the most beautiful boy ever except for two things:

1. He barely comes up to my shoulders.

2. He will not shut up. (That's when I knew for sure

that I hadn't done a thing with him. I never went for the talkers.)

These honors kids have everything so fucking easy. In English, for example, our assignment was to sit in groups and discuss our thoughts about a novel. That's a class?

Please. It was just like study hall, only more boring.

Anyway, Mel ended up in my group. The bitch girl from history was there too. Mel called her "Caro," and as soon as he said it I realized I did know her.

Julia and I used to be friends with her.

Back in middle school, we hung out with Caro for a while. Or, as J called her, Corn Syrup. I can't remember when Julia came up with the name, but it fit. And still did.

She gave me a look as I sat down but (obviously) didn't speak to me. The last person in the group was the other guy who'd stared at me in history. He didn't say anything to me or anyone else, just looked at his desk until Mel said, "Patrick, what do you think?"

Patrick looked up, shrugged, and then glanced at me before staring at his desk again. That's when I realized that while I hadn't messed around with Mel, I had definitely hooked up with Patrick.

He looked at me and all this stuff I thought I'd forgotten came roaring back.

I got through the rest of class by staring at the wall and thinking about how me and Julia used to go to that twenty-four-hour pancake place after parties and eat chocolate chip pancakes and drink coffee until our waitress would come by and say, "So, are you going to pay your check or what?"

As soon as the bell rang I went to the nurse's office and faked cramps. They called Mom, who called Dad, who called the school back and asked to talk to me. He said, "I called Laurie and she said you really need to stick it out." A pause. "Honey."

Yes, Dad has taken to trying endearments on me. It's not working. It's obvious he's only ever said them to Mom and it makes him feel weird to use them on anyone else.

"Fine," I said, and hung up. Stupid Laurie. I thought shrinks were supposed to help you, not torture you.

The nurse should have sent me back to class then but she didn't. That was nice of her.

I should have guessed something bad would happen.

She told me to lie back down and got me a cup of water. When I was done with it she started telling me about her oldest son and how he was in Pinewood once too. Then she said, "You know, I remember seeing you and Julia—" and before she could say another word I told her I was feeling better and left.

I only had one class to get through after that. It was physics, which dropped me back in with the honors kids again. Also more group work, this time solving some problem involving rolling metal balls through some contraption and then measuring stuff. No one would let me touch anything, which was fine with me. I just sat there, and then some girl said, "Are you sure you're supposed to be in this class?"

I tried to do that freeze-you-out thing Julia would do when she was mad. She'd turn away and act like whoever spoke didn't exist. It worked on guys pretty well, even Kevin, and the two times she did it to me I begged her to talk to me again after less than ten seconds.

But my attempt at it? It didn't work. I turned away too fast and caught my hip on the table with a nice hard smack. I acted like I didn't notice my clumsiness (or the pain), ignored all the snickers at my table, and looked around the room. I actually recognized a lot of the kids from parties. They just look different when they aren't messed up. Less human.

Mel nodded at me when I saw him and said something to Patrick, who pushed a pencil around in his hands and then stared out the window. Mel sighed, gave me a small half smile, and then went back to work. Patrick kept staring out the window, even when someone at the table next to his said something, making sure my name and those of a few guys were loud enough for me to hear. As if I didn't already know I had a reputation. Please. I worked hard for it.

I have this theory about sex. I never told Julia about it because . . . well, because I just came up with it today as I sat in that stupid class. But I think it's pretty good. And I think Julia would have liked it.

This is my theory:

If you sleep with one guy—well, who cares? Nobody. It actually generates less talk than if you're a virgin.

Two guys—same deal, unless you do both of them in the same night and are stupid enough to let someone take pictures. (Stephanie Foster!)

Once you get past two, the number of guys you sleep with gets more complicated. Say you sleep with three guys. Everyone will know you slept with ten and talk a lot of crap about you.

Four guys means people think you've slept with so many that every drunk or high (or both) guy will talk to you at parties because, hey, you put out for anyone.

Past four? You're a pathetic, diseased slut and everyone knows it, so the only guys you can get are the loser ones, and even then they'll never call and always wear a condom because—well, look where you've been!

That's why five is the perfect number. You get left alone and if you do feel like doing something (which I don't—getting to five was enough work, thank you), you can find someone stupid and forgettable and it won't turn into drama. Or a relationship. (Which is really the same thing.)

I wish I could have told Julia this. She would have loved it. She would have had a shirt made that said "pathetic slut" in sequins. She would have worn it too, and laughed her ass off at anyone who said something.

I've been with five and a half guys. I always told Julia five. I didn't—I didn't talk about the half. Not even with her.

Patrick was the half. It happened at a party in Millertown late last spring, the one Julia decided we should go to because she was fighting with Kevin and hoped he'd be there.

He wasn't and so she had some acid and then got pissed at me because I wouldn't, waved me away when I reminded her that acid always freaked me out and that I was fine, I had the vodka we'd picked up beforehand.

"You won't even drink unless you get to open the bottle," she said, her voice soft but her words sharp, slicing me open in the way only she could. "You're such a control freak."

I stumbled back, hurt by the anger in her voice, and she sighed and threw her arms around me, said, "God, Amy, come on, have some fun. Let go a little! Live!"

And then she whirled away, caught up in the party. She didn't look back.

I drank my vodka, trying to get up the nerve to find her, but it didn't work. The world was blurred the way I liked, but I didn't feel relaxed and safe. I felt too tall and stupid, out of place. Everyone around me was having fun, but I wasn't.

I felt like I should have been having fun but I knew, deep down, that I never would. Not the way Julia could. I could never just let go. It sucked, but it's how things were for me. Plus I hated knowing Julia was mad at me. So I left the party and went outside to wait in her car.

I tripped over someone as I was walking down the porch steps. A guy, sitting there with a mostly full cup of beer by his side. He was staring off into the distance, arms wrapped around his legs. He looked as unhappy as I felt.

"Sorry," I said automatically.

"My fault," he said, and then, "Are you all right?"

"I'm fine," I said, another automatic response, and he said, "Okay," and stood up. When he did, his hand touched mine, and I felt something, a strange, sudden jolt inside me.

I used to act annoyed whenever Julia talked about Kevin and how she felt a spark every time he touched her, but the truth was I knew exactly what she meant after that night. I just never told her.

He must have felt that jolt too because he said, "Oh," quietly. Almost startled.

We ended up in the basement, jimmied open a sliding glass door and went inside. It was dark and unfinished, a single bare lightbulb shedding a tiny ring of light onto the sagging sofa we sat on. We didn't talk much. His name was Patrick. I said, "I'm Amy," and waited for the usual crap about how he'd seen me around before. Instead he looked at the floor and said, "You hang out with that girl, Julia, right?"

"Yeah."

"I thought so. I don't go to many parties."

"Yeah? I go to a lot."

He nodded and then looked at me. There was something almost frightened in his eyes. It was weird, but it . . . I don't know. It made me really look at him, not just as some random guy, but as a person.

"It's lonely, don't you think?" he said, gesturing around the room. It was all bare walls and exposed beams. Even the spiderwebs in the corners of the ceiling were dusty, like they'd been abandoned. One of his fingers brushed against my arm and I felt that spark again. It was like part of me had been asleep until that moment. Like somehow, I'd been waiting for something I hadn't even known about.

"It looks safe," I said, honest like I never was with guys, spinning on that spark, and the fright in his eyes melted into something else, something like understanding. If he'd tried to kiss me then, nothing important would have happened. We would have had sex and that would have been it. But he didn't try to kiss me. He just leaned over and pushed my hair back with one hand, tucking it behind my ears. Guys did that to Julia all the time because her hair was long and honey-colored, beautiful. Mine is short and the color red leaves are right before they rot.

"Why did you do that?" I said.

"I wanted to," he said, and looked so surprised, like wanting was brand new to him, that I kissed him.

I'd kissed guys before that, kissed guys after that. They were all the same. They were nothing. But I remember that kiss; the strange rightness of it, the taste of his mouth, shockingly raw without the layers of smoke and alcohol I was used to.

He touched me like I expected, which was fine, the clumsy peeling away of my clothes and the hitch in his breathing when I tucked my hands in his shirt and pushed it up over his head. It felt better than usual though, touching him and having him touch me, and that made me feel strange. Anxious. But I didn't pull away. That damn spark, that pull I felt when our hands had touched—it kept me there.

I'd always picked skinny guys before, guys who were all bones and angles. Guys who were small in my arms, guys I could see around. Patrick was solid, and instead of ribs and shoulder blades, I felt muscle rippling under his skin. It should have felt strange, but it didn't. I couldn't even see around him, but I didn't care. He was rubbing against me, still in his jeans, and it felt so good I couldn't bring myself to reach for his zipper and move things along. My skin felt too hot and too tight in a way it hadn't ever before, and I dug my fingernails into his shoulders, unable to really think but somehow sure something was going to happen. And then it did.

It's the only time it has, despite what I said to Julia when she got pissed at me after I told her there was no way the orgasms she had with Kevin were worth putting up with walking in on some girl blowing him. She said I'd never understand, and how could I since I only screwed guys who were too stupid to know girls could have them? I had to lie to her then, if only so I could make my point.

I wish I hadn't now.

I wish I could have told her she was right about the guys I picked. I wish I could have told her that having one scared the shit out of me.

I pushed and then shoved at Patrick till I was free, getting up and throwing on my clothes as I rushed out the door we'd snuck through. I looked back once. I don't know why I did. He was just sitting there, staring after me, and I saw his bewildered face, the tiny marks I'd left on the tops of his shoulders. I saw him and I wanted to go back.

I never wanted that, not ever, no matter how much I drank, and so I ran. I ran as fast as I could. I went to Julia's car, got in and locked the doors. I curled into the backseat, into the dark.

J found me later, like she always did, and said she was sorry for earlier.

"What have you been doing?" she said, and I lied to her.

"Nothing," I said. "I've just been here."

I'm sorry about that now. I just didn't think she'd understand. Sex was always something Julia hoped would lead to more, to really being with someone.

I never wanted it to lead to anything. I had sex when I was drunk because it was a way to be close to someone without really being close at all. I know what people say about it, the physical and emotional intimacy of sex and whatever, but less than a minute of latex-covered flesh inside me isn't intimate. It's not even skin touching skin.

I don't know why I'm thinking about this. About Patrick. It happened ages ago and it doesn't matter. I just feel so awful about this whole stupid day and all my stupid classes, and I have to get up and do it again tomorrow and the day after that and the day after that and—

I just called Julia's house. I had to. I didn't say anything when her mother answered. I couldn't find the right words, couldn't find any words, but I guess she knew it was me. She told me she hoped I was proud of myself.

She said, "How does it feel to know you've taken someone's life?" I don't know if she meant herself or Julia's. Maybe she meant both.

I said, "I'm sorry," the words finally starting to come, but it was too late. She'd already hung up and I spoke to silence. To no one.

88 days

J,

Things aren't going back to how they've always been at home, and it's kind of freaking me out. Not "going to take a drink" freaking me out, though I suppose if I knew how to do drama right I'd be doing exactly that. But then I never did know how to do drama, did I? No matter how gone I was, I never confronted my parents or danced on tables. I just slumped onto sofas or chairs at parties and nodded at people or talked to you. I had sex five times—three times in ninth grade, twice last year. (I know what you're thinking, and yes, I know you know about Patrick now, because I bet you know everything, and yes, I should have told you, but I don't want to get into that again. Okay?)

When I first got to Pinewood and had to talk about the things I did while "under the influence," I got these looks, these "That's your story? That's all you did?" looks.

They went away when I talked about you. What I did.

The thing at home is that my parents keep talking to me and it's—well, it's weird. I don't know how to talk to them. I alternate between wanting to scream at them for not caring enough to do it sooner and wanting to tell them everything.

Everything, J. I want to tell them it's too late and why. I want to tell them I feel lost. I want to tell them how creepy it is to be in classes with the grade-obsessed freaks. It sucks that you had to die before they realized that maybe they should try talking to their own kid once in a while.

Let me illustrate the weirdness. This was the conversation I had with my mother yesterday after she drove me home from school:

Mom: [calling] Amy. [long pause] Honey. (Apparently, she's trying to get the hang of the endearment thing too.) Where are you? Maybe we should talk about your—oh. You're in the kitchen.

Yours Truly: Yeah. Remember, we came in here about five minutes ago? You watched me sit down and said you were going to put your bag away?

Mom: Of course! I just thought you might have gone up to your room.

YT: Oh, I can. I mean, I will. Just let me get my stuff and—

Mom: No, no, stay. [sits down] How was your day?

YT: Um. Fine.

Mom: How are your classes?

YT: Fine.

Mom: Are you working on homework?

YT: Yeah.

Mom: Are you—how is it going? I know it must seem like a lot of work. Not that I don't think you can't handle the work, but—

YT: It's fine.

Mom [visibly relieved]: Oh, good. I feel like a snack. Do you want a bologna sandwich? I'm going to have one. [stands up]

YT: I'm a vegetarian. Have been since I was thirteen.

Mom: Oh . . . I didn't . . . I've seen you pick pepperoni off pizza but I didn't think it meant anything— I mean, I didn't realize you were so committed. I think that's great, really, and—

YT: Thanks. I'm just going to grab my stuff and go upstairs.

I did, and the thing is, Mom looked so sad, standing there in the kitchen all alone. Like she . . . I don't know. Wanted me to stay and talk to her? But if that was true, why didn't she just say it? I think you know why she didn't. She felt bad for the mess she and Dad made. It wasn't really about me at all.

But still, J. That look. It made me feel horrible. It made me feel something else too, something that left a bitter taste in my mouth and cramped my hands into fists.

See, now everything I do is worth noticing. Now the things I do mean something to them. Now, when what I've done is all I can see when I look at myself in the mirror.

Then there's school. As long as I avoid your locker, it's okay. Sort of.

Okay, not really. It sucks. Obviously, I'm not hanging out with the people we used to. Just looking at them makes me think of you and, well, I can't handle it. Plus . . . J, they avoid me. I don't blame them. I wouldn't talk to any of them after what happened or even at your funeral. I went to Pinewood this summer, not parties. I was there when you died.

I'm the reason you're gone.

So no old friends. And no new ones among my dumb-ass honors classmates either, which, frankly, is fine with me, as I'm not interested in hanging out with people who have poles shoved up their butts. However—and I know you'll find this amusing—Corn Syrup Caro has actually spoken to me! We were sitting in our groups in English class when someone across the room mentioned your name, and I just . . . I zoned out or something. Freaked out, I guess. My brain just kinda went *pzzzt*, and my face got all hot, and it was like I couldn't hear or think or anything. I was dimly aware of Mel glancing at me and then at Patrick (who, as always, was staring at his desk, though I think he might have looked at me). But Caro actually said something. She said, "Amy, are you okay? Do you need some water or—" but then Beth Emory sneered at me and Corn Syrup shut up. She hasn't spoken to me since.

You remember Beth Emory, right? Another middle school nightmare. She's still exactly the same. Gorgeous, mean, and able to say things that make her friends act like frightened little sheep. Baaaaa. Of course Caro still hangs out with her.

There is actually one person who does talk to me. It's that guy, Mel. In English class, when we're stuck in that stupid group, he's always asking me questions. "What's your favorite color?" or "How come you dropped psychology to take environmental science?" Stuff like that. It's weird, because while he seems to know an awful lot about me—like my schedule, for instance—and is always asking stuff, he doesn't seem all that interested in the answers. I can't figure him out, but since I don't care it works out fine.

You know what my biggest problem with school is? Lunch. I didn't expect that. In Pinewood we had to do a lot of role-playing (I know!), and I was always fine with "learning to be by myself." But at school it's different. Who sits where, with whom, and why, matters. It matters a lot, and the fact that I don't have anyone to sit with—well, you know what that makes me.

There's a couple of other kids who eat by themselves, but I'm in no mood for a very special episode moment, and even if I was it still wouldn't be enough to make me sit with the girl who needs to be told to bleach her mustache or the guy who always wears a suit and tie. I suppose he's making a real fashion statement, but this is high school. You're not supposed to be real. You're supposed to be enough like everyone else to get through and out into the waiting world.

FIVE

SCHOOL STARTED OFF normally enough; annoying classes, annoying people. The usual. And then came lunch.

It was the same as always at first. I bought fries and a soda, and then grabbed a seat at the far end of the freshman reject table. The rejects—all pimples and desperation—gawked at me. I heard one of them whisper "Julia," and thought of her sitting outside my house waiting for me in the morning, drinking coffee from the convenience store and picking the foam cup apart. She always made it "snow" when I got in the car, and for a second it was just like it used to be, me buckling my seat belt, yawning, and her laughing as little pieces of foam fell down on us. I felt my eyes get all prickly hot and stared at my fries.

Then someone sat down across from me. I was sure it was that fat girl with the mustache, and I know I'm supposed to be kind to my fellow losers, but screw that. I know they look at me and see exactly what I see when I look at them. They see someone who can't find one person to eat lunch with. They see a loser. That's what I am. That's what mustache girl is too, and well, if there's a reason no one wants to hang out with me . . . it's not that hard to figure out why she's alone too, is it?

It wasn't her, though. It was freaking Corn Syrup Caro with a tray full of diet soda and lettuce and her cute little purse. I dropped the fry I was holding.

"I thought maybe you might want to go over the physics notes from yesterday," she said. Her face was bright red, and her hands were shaking. I looked around the cafeteria. It took me a second to find her table—it's on the other side, where the people who have some social standing are allowed to sit. Her friends were giggling, and Beth was eating salad and looking smug. I knew what was going on right away.

Before Julia, Beth and her dopey band of losers were my "friends," which meant Beth was always getting mad at me and making me do stuff to prove I was sorry or worse, doing stuff to make me sorry for whatever it was I'd done wrong. In fourth grade she made me sit by myself on the way home from a field trip to the aquarium while she and Caro and Anne Alice put crap in my hair. I still remember feeling Caro rub cupcake into my scalp.

Today I got to be the crap in Caro's hair.

"How long do you have to stay before Beth forgives you?" I asked. Caro's face got even redder.

"I'm not—" she said, and looked over at her table. Beth gave her a tight smile and then turned away just enough for me and Caro to see her say something. "I just thought you might want some help catching up." Over at Beth's table, everyone laughed again.

"Can I ask you something?"

"Sure." She tried a smile, failed, and twisted her fork around in her salad really hard, spraying wilted lettuce and carrot into the air. Her face got even redder. I almost felt sorry for her, but then remembered she chose to hang out with someone who treated her like dirt.

So I said, "Did you have a choice? Like was it me or the nose picker or mustache girl, or am I the ultimate punishment? Talk to the girl whose best friend is dead and—"

"No one thinks it's your fault," Caro said quickly, too quickly.

I choked even though there was nothing in my mouth, my throat closing up tight around her words. The room went blurry around me, my vision tunneling, and I pushed away from the table.

The thing is, I know people know what happened. I do. I know everyone looks at me and sees death scrawled across my skin. It was just weird to have someone finally say it. It hurt a lot more than I thought it would, this weird grinding twist in my chest, like my heart wanted to stop beating but couldn't. Wouldn't. I looked over at the mustache girl. She was staring but quickly looked away as our eyes met. Clearly I'd overestimated my social standing.

"I'm sorry," Caro said even more quickly. "Don't go. Please. I have to talk to you for five minutes."

I know what Julia would have done. She would have dumped her fries on Caro's head and walked off. But I looked at her, so miserable and so clearly desperate to make her friend (admittedly, a friend who is pure evil, but still) talk to her again, and I could get that. I mean, I always hated it when Julia was mad at me. So I sat back down.

She actually talked about physics. I thought we'd sit in silence but I guess Beth told her to talk and Caro figured physics would be easiest or something. The funny thing is, she was happy talking about it. Like, her face lit up, and she was smiling, and when I asked her questions she really started talking. Caro's a lot smarter—at least about physics—than she lets on because she started talking about stuff we've barely touched on in class. Halfway through her explanation of measuring the speed of light we got into a conversation about time travel (I know how it sounds, but it really is kind of interesting) and before I knew it lunch was over. Surprised the hell out of me. Corn Syrup too. The bell rang and her eyes got huge. She looked around for Beth and started to race off. And then she hesitated, just for a second, like we were going to keep talking.

She bolted, of course, but I was surprised she'd stopped for even that moment.

SIX

TODAY WAS A LAURIE DAY TOO—as if I hadn't dealt with enough crap with Caro and lunch already. I'd hoped to miss school to see Laurie, but naturally she has afternoon hours for her "teen" patients. Lucky, lucky me. Mom, thankfully, had to do some grocery shopping and just dropped me off. I wasn't up for a discussion about "how things are going" with her while I was stuck in the waiting room.

Eventually, I guess Laurie must have somehow known I'd looked through all the magazines twice and was contemplating bolting and had me called back.

She started off normally enough—for her, anyway, with the "How are you feeling?" questions and all that crap. But then she said, "Today I want to talk about Julia."

"Okay, well, it's been ninety days today," I said, because telling Laurie to shut the hell up doesn't work. I've tried it.

"No," she said. "I mean, tell me about her."

"Well, the accident—"

"No, before that. When did you first meet?"

"She moved here when she was twelve."

Laurie was silent. She does that sometimes. I can never tell if it's because I've said something wrong or because she's thinking. Either way, I always end up babbling.

"I was eleven." See? Babbling. Does Laurie really care when I met Julia? Highly doubtful.

"What did Julia think about your drinking?" And once again, I was right. She'd gone right for the drinking. So predictable.

I stared at her, annoyed. She stared right back.

"Well, if it hadn't been for . . . if it hadn't been for that night, for me, she never would have—"

"Let's not talk about that right now," Laurie said. "You drank before the accident, right?"

"Yes."

"A lot?"

I shrugged. It wasn't like we hadn't talked about this before.

But she kept quiet again, so I finally said, "Yeah, a lot."

"When did you drink?"

"Before parties, at parties. Weekend stuff. Last year, though, I drank at school sometimes."

"Why parties? Why sometimes at school?"

I made a face at her because, really, how stupid could she be? Even I know I drank because it made me feel okay about having weird red hair and being so tall. It also made me less nervous about acting like an idiot in front of other people, and parties and school were times when I desperately didn't want to seem stupid. Drinking made me feel so much better about—well, everything.

"Amy, I know we've covered this before, but I think we should talk about it again. Let me ask another question," Laurie said, as if I could stop her. "What sort of things did you do to keep your parents from noticing you took alcohol from them?"

"My parents don't drink." I knew she had all this in her little file or chart or whatever. My first week at Pinewood I talked and talked and talked about all this crap, and she was in the room when I did. (And she had her damn pen.)

Laurie didn't say anything, though, just gave me her interested look (You'd think they'd learn more than one expression in shrink school), so I sighed and recited what we both already knew.

"My mom had a cousin who died from alcohol poisoning when he was twenty-two. My dad's aunt was an alcoholic. Why don't you just say you want me to ask them about my dead drunk relatives?"

"Right now, I really would like to focus on you. How did you drink?"

I rolled my eyes and opened my mouth, holding up a pretend bottle.

She clicked her pen twice. I hate that damn thing.

"Julia would swipe stuff from her mom or find someone who'd buy for us."

"So she drank too?"

"Sure, if there was nothing else around."

"And if there was?"

"If there was what?"

"If there was something else around?"

"Then she'd do that."

"I see," Laurie said, and the minute she did I knew where she was going and it pissed me the hell off.

"Julia didn't like how much I drank, you know. Like, if I'd puke she'd say I should think about cutting back, and that it was stupid to drink when I could just do something that wouldn't make me totally sick like drop aci . . . um. Anyway, she had to look out for me. And she did. But I—I didn't do a very good job of looking out for her."

She nodded. "For next time, I want you to think about talking about Julia. Not about the accident. Just about her. What she was like. How you met, the kind of things you did together. Would you be willing to do that?"

"I guess."

After that we talked about the usual stuff we do when Laurie says we're "wrapping up"—do I want to drink, what do I do when I want to drink, a review of my "coping skills," blah blah blah. I swear I could tell Laurie I'd just murdered someone and she'd still make me review what I've "learned."

Here's the thing about that: how often I want to drink doesn't seem to be a big deal to her. How can it not be? Look at what I did, at what my drinking cost . . . how can I even think about it at all?

But I do.

I also told her a little about lunch. I don't know why, because she said she thought I should try to "strike up a conversation" with Corn Syrup. Yeah, okay, great idea.

Laurie really doesn't get how high school works, but that's how adults are. They think school is so easy and life there is so great. I'd like to see them go back.

Laurie wouldn't last a day.

99 days

Well, J, it's Friday night. Are you ready to hear my exciting plans?

My parents have asked me to join them while they watch some special on the History Channel. So I'm here in the living room, lying on the floor and working on homework. You know, I haven't actually done homework in ages. You and I had, what, two study halls last year? I don't remember ever opening a book in either of them. I remember you painting your fingernails and mine. I remember talking about Kevin and your mom and my parents. I remember making plans for after school, for the weekend. It was so great when your mom gave you a car (even with the lecture about how much she sacrificed for you) and we didn't have to take the bus everywhere.

Remember when we decided what we were going to do once we were done with high school? We'd bailed on lunch to smoke in the third-floor bathroom, and I drank a ton of those little bottles you kept in your locker because Mom and Dad had actually fought that morning and it was all horrible silence until Mom started to cry. Then Dad put his arms around her and it was like I wasn't even there even though we were all in the kitchen, and worse than the rare fight was the all-too-regular sight of them so wrapped up in each other that they forgot I was there.

We decided the day after we graduated we were going to move to Millertown—out of Lawrenceville, finally! — and get an apartment. You were going to help out with Kevin's band, and I was . . . whoa. Déjà vu.

It's . . . J, it's so strong I feel almost sick. Have you ever felt memory like this? It's like I'm there with you smiling and waving at me, your fingernails painted pink and red and blue and green. I might have been drunk then, floating through life, but it was real. I was real. You were real. This crap—lying on the floor, this stupid homework, all of it—it feels like nothing. It is nothing.

Me again.

Mom and Dad have finally let me out of their sight to go to bed. It was pretty obvious something was wrong with me because I couldn't stand another moment of their stupid show about some stupid guy who built churches, and I got up and—well, I got up and just stood there, shaking. I stood there because I wanted a drink and hated myself for it. I hated myself for wanting it because it took me back to that night, to that quiet road, to the way I lay shivering in the ambulance, cold even though I shouldn't have been, surrounded by people hovering over me but without the one person I most wanted to see.

My parents talked and talked, said all the things I suppose Laurie and Pinewood taught them to say. The truth, J, the truth I know you already know, is that their talking isn't what stopped me. Pinewood isn't what keeps me from drinking either. It never has been. The reason I don't drink is because of what happened to you. What I did.

I tried once, the morning after you died. I rolled out of bed, rested against the floor until I felt strong enough to stand. I found a bottle in my bottom dresser drawer. I went to pick it up and saw your face, heard you crying and me promising everything would be all right. I opened the bottle, and you stared at me, eyes open and glitter dusted across your cheekbones. I took a sip, and I could see out the ambulance window. You were lying on the ground, your hands open wide, holding on to nothing. There were people standing over you, looking down at you, and I knew you'd never see them.

I couldn't swallow. I opened up the attic window, gagging, then grabbed the bottle and tossed it as far as I could. That afternoon my parents started talking about Pinewood. They started talking about it more when I said, "Fine. Whatever. I don't care."

I thought about killing myself the day after your funeral. I was in my room, behind the locked attic door staring at the picture we had taken the time we skipped school and went to Adventure Park. Remember that? You talked that guy into letting us in for free and we rode on all the rides and bought a picture of ourselves smiling with someone in a squirrel suit. I knew Dad kept a bottle of sleeping pills in the medicine cabinet in the bathroom he shares with Mom, for the times he's overseas and has to sleep because he has an early meeting about whatever merger his company is working on. They wouldn't have noticed till it was too late.

You know why I didn't do it? It wasn't because I didn't want to. I did. God, I did. I didn't because living with what I'd done to you was what I deserved. I deserved to be alone. I deserved the shaking and the headaches and the fact that every single time I took a breath I felt a squeezing in my chest, my heart beating even though I wished it wasn't.

I deserve to live like this now, to have tonight happen to me. I deserve to remember the way things were and realize they're gone. That I destroyed them. I won't drink and let myself wipe it away for a little while.

When Mom and Dad were done talking tonight they made me sit between them on the sofa. Dad fiddled with the remote and patted my knee. Mom put an arm around my shoulders, squeezing gently every once in a while. We watched a movie, something with wacky misunderstandings and an ending where everything turned out okay. I could tell because there was happy music. It was a very long eighty-seven minutes.

"You did it," Mom said as the credits rolled. Dad said, "Amy, we're so proud of you." It made me happy to hear them say that, and I don't deserve that either. I always wanted family stuff like this. It's kind of funny, isn't it? All those years of great grades when I was young, all those years of trying to squeeze into their world, and it turns out I just needed to stop caring, become a drunk who dragged her best friend into a car and—

I can't stand this, you being gone. I'm so sorry, J. You don't know how sorry I am for what happened. For what I did.

I know they're just words. But I mean them, I swear. I'm sorry. Please forgive me everything.

SEVEN

I TOLD JULIA about tonight, but I didn't—I didn't tell her about school. I tried, staring at the paper, pen in my hand, but the words wouldn't come. I don't want . . .

I don't want her to know what I saw today.

I was at my locker at the end of school, grabbing my stuff. Everyone was talking, planning their weekends and discussing what we're all supposed to care about, who did what to who and why.

I shut my locker, and Kevin was standing there. Rich, his stupid-ass best friend and the last guy I slept with— number five and the biggest waste of my time because he actually tried to act like my boyfriend afterward till I had to tell him to get lost—was standing a few feet away, acting like I wasn't there. That didn't surprise me.

I was actually surprised either of them would come near me at all.

"Hi," Kevin said.

He really said that. "Hi." Like it was just another Friday and not ninety-nine days since Julia had strode down the hall and said, "God, I'm so glad to be free of this place till September!" Like it wasn't ninety-nine days since she'd died.

I stared at him.

"I want to show you something," Kevin said, and pushed up his sleeve. He had a tattoo spiraling around his wrist. Julia's name, written out dark and forever.

"She'd love it," he said, and put a hand on my arm. He sounded so sure.

I wanted to take his face in my hands and pull. I wanted to rip off his skin, tear it to shreds, and leave him broken. Julia's name on his wrist, like it would fix what happened, like it could ever fix what happened: Julia's swollen red eyes, her sobbing as we stood in someone's house, and him staring stone-faced, not even calling her name as we left.

I know what I did to her, and I know—I know I have no right to talk. But I hate him. God, I hate him.

"I really loved her, you know," Kevin said, as if I'd commented on his tattoo, as if I'd spoken. "I loved her so much. And now—" His voice broke, his eyes filled with tears, and I saw girls walking by look at him, sympathy and lust on their faces, and maybe he does miss Julia, maybe now he loves her like she always wanted. But that—that writing Julia won't ever see, those tears and regret she didn't get until it was too late—the wrongness of it made me want to scream.

I pushed his hand off my arm. He gave me a dark look and smeared over it with a smile. "I forgive you for what you did, you know."

My vision went dark, spotted red and hazy. I shoved past him, his predictable muttering ("Be that way, bitch") washing over me and making the red haze I saw beat like a second heart. Rich said something to me too, as if I would care what he thought, as if sex with him once (for thirty-seven whole seconds) meant something. All I could think about was Julia. Her shattered face after she saw Kevin with that other girl. My hand on her arm, guiding her away. Leading her to the car.

I wanted to get away and couldn't. I was trapped in the school, in walking past the thing her locker had been turned into. I was paying for telling her we should leave the party, I would always be paying. I bumped into someone just as I heard Mel say, "Hey, watch where— Hey, Amy, you okay?"

I blinked, confused, and saw Mel watching me from a few feet away. I didn't understand. How could he be over there when I'd just bumped into him?

I hadn't. I'd walked into Patrick. He just hadn't said anything. I looked at him and he—he was looking at me. He looked at me like no one, not even Laurie, has. He looked at me like he could see everything, all the way down into the rotten places inside me.

I didn't like that. I hated it. I hated him. I hated everyone, everything. I wanted to rip the whole world apart so it wouldn't be like this anymore. Patrick blinked and something passed through his eyes, a curious understanding. He didn't say a word.

I pushed past him and went outside to wait for Mom, but I could still see that tattoo, see Julia's name. I could still hear Kevin saying how much he loved Julia when she wasn't around to hear it. I could still see Patrick looking at me, and I knew none of it would go away.

I knew I'd remember it all.

104 days

Hey J,

It's Wednesday, but that doesn't matter. All my days are the same.

I:

Get up, eat breakfast with Mom. Read encouraging note left by Dad, who has to leave early every morning because his company is in talks with another company in the UK and he's having all these teleconferences. Take shower. Get dressed. Look in mirror. Still freakishly tall. Hair still the shade of red that makes people (usually old) say things like "My, it looks like someone lit a match on your head!" I miss you telling those people to watch out or they'd get burned.

Mom calls out that we're "almost very late" and

drives me to school. So far this week I have learned that Mom:

— hates chairing the curriculum committee she's on because the proposed changes won't attract more students into art classes.

— is "very proud" of my being a vegetarian and has ordered some "yummy" cookbooks. I told her she could let me know how they tasted. She laughed. I can't remember the last time I made anyone do that.

School is locker, class, no time for locker, class, rush to locker, barely make it to class—you get the idea. Of course there's still lunch too. The past few days I've caught Corn Syrup looking at me a couple of times. For someone allowed to bask in Beth's glow (ha!), Corn Syrup usually looks pretty miserable. Beth has probably gotten angry with her for having split ends or something.

After school I get a ride home with either Dad or Mom. Because the UK thing is going pretty well, Dad has been able to make it so he works at home in the afternoon every other week. This week he's home, so he picks me up.

Things Dad likes to talk about:
—Tennis
—How my day was
—Tennis

I'm starting to think the reason my parents are so in love is that they both realize they are so boring no one else could stand being with them.

At home I continue the excitement and work on homework. My grades are good so far, but I'm not sure I get the point of the whole studying thing. Take English, for instance. We're reading *The Scarlet Letter* and all anyone talks about in class is what's-her-name and her big red *A*.

I find myself wondering what Pearl's going to be like when she grows up.

Oh, and get this—Mom and Dad got rid of my computer. It's so I can "focus on my studies," but hello, I was the one in Pinewood, and I sat through all the lectures about the "dangers" of "falling back in with old friends and habits." Anyway, now I have to type my papers and do research in the study, which (of course) is where whoever has taken me home has camped out. I thought about telling Mom and Dad that the only person I ever talked to online was you, but the computer in the study is nicer. Mine always sounded like it was powered by a hamster running around in one of those little wheels.

After I study, it's dinnertime. Mom and Dad cook together, and you'd think I'd get a break then, but nope. I "help" by stirring stuff. There was a weird moment the other day when I was eating baby carrots and hoping my arm wasn't going to fall off from stirring some rice dish and Mom said, "You know, I could never get you to touch a carrot when you were younger."

I said, "Well, I guess things changed when my teeth came in or something," and she looked shocked for a second, and then she looked sort of pissed off. Like it's my fault she never noticed what I ate before? She was grating cheese, and she slammed the block of it down on the counter, saying, "I was simply trying to talk to you. There isn't any need to—"

"What? Point out the obvious? You didn't even know I was a vegetarian."

Her face fell, and she picked up the cheese again, staring at it and blinking hard. Dad touched Mom's arm and said, "Grace," gently, sharing a look with her before he turned to me and said, "So, how's that rice looking?"

"Kind of gloopy," I said.

He smiled, and then she did, but I could tell I'd rattled Mom, that she'd realized that not only did she not know that her kid was around or that she was drinking, but that she didn't even know I ate carrots. And that I knew she knew nothing about me.

I liked that.

I liked that she had to see that, J. And I like that every day brings a whole lot of time with my parents. I know how it sounds, okay? But I like that it's not them and then me anymore.

I like that they finally have to face the fact that I'm here.

EIGHT

IN ENGLISH CLASS TODAY (109 days without Julia—I can only measure time by that, by how long she's been gone), I got stuck in yet another group thing with Mel and Caro and Patrick. We were still discussing *The Scarlet Letter*, and I watched Corn Syrup twirl a piece of her hair around one finger as she argued with Mel. So far, they'd argued about what the *A* really meant (I hadn't realized that was up for debate) and then the symbolism of the color red. I'd drawn squares in my notebook. Patrick had fiddled with his book, then picked his fingernails, and then fiddled with his book some more.

Then—and this is where things started to get strange— Mel looked at Patrick and cleared his throat. Patrick stopped picking his fingernails and glared at him. Watching them do that reminded me of how Julia and I used to talk without words. I started thinking about her and then Mel sighed, turned to me, and said, "What are you doing Friday night?"

"What?" I said, completely thrown and positive I hadn't heard him right.

I had, though, because Caro stopped the hair twirling so fast her finger got caught and she had to yank it free. And Patrick was—well, he was fiddling with his book again.

"Maybe we could go to a movie," Mel continued. "I was thinking that you and me and maybe . . ." He cleared his throat again and then, I swear, flinched like someone had kicked him or something.

He glared at Patrick and then looked back at me. "You wanna go?"

"Um," I said, and realized that:

1. At sixteen, I was finally getting asked out on an honest-to-God date.

2. I was asked on said date by someone who, as far as I could tell, wasn't even interested in me. Mel never checked out my (admittedly small) chest, tried to grope me, or even seemed interested in my answers to the questions he was always asking.

3. I was clearly taking too long to reply because Caro was staring at me and Mel like we both had two heads.

Mel was blinking a lot and had turned bright red, and Patrick had actually stopped flipping through his book and was watching all of us.

I knew I had to say something, but I had no idea what. I tried to think of the right thing, but nothing came to mind and I panicked.

I panicked, and said the worst possible thing.

I panicked and said, "When?"

"Friday," Caro snapped. "He said Friday."

"Caro," Mel said, glancing at her. He looked upset.

"What?" Caro said, her voice full of challenge and hurt, and she looked about ten times more upset then Mel did.

Mel opened his mouth, then closed it. His face was still bright red. I didn't get what was going on, but it was clear I needed to say something else.

"Okay," I said. I meant it as, "Okay, I understand you mean Friday, now will you please explain what the hell is going on?" but Mel must have taken my "okay" as a "yes" because he nodded at me.

"Great, I'll see you then," he said, and then looked at Caro and told her he didn't agree with what she'd said about Reverend What's-His-Bucket.

After a moment of extremely awkward silence Caro said, "Of course you'd say that, because you didn't read the book right," and then they started arguing again.

I spent the rest of class trying to figure out why the hell I was going on a date with Mel, who was hot but short and clearly more than a little strange. Patrick flipped through his book and picked his fingernails. No surprise there. Caro and Mel kept arguing. No surprise there either.

When the bell rang, I'd decided that I'd probably hallucinated the whole thing out of sheer boredom, but then Mel said, "I'll pick you up around seven, okay?" and then, "Ow," as Patrick accidentally elbowed him in the head in his rush to get out of his desk.

I nodded in Mel's direction just so I could get out of there and then spent all of my next class totally pissed at myself for being so . . . well, me. But then I realized Mel doesn't know where I live, so maybe this dating thing will work out after all.

NINE

TODAY ME AND LAURIE were supposed to talk about Julia. She said that last time. I know she did. I heard her. And Laurie—

I really fucking hate her.

Things started out okay.

"How do I start?" I said after we'd done the introductory bullshit. I didn't know how to put Julia into words. She was bigger than that.

"However you want," Laurie said. So helpful, as always.

I started at the beginning. "I met Julia when I was eleven. I had just started sixth grade. Mom and Dad had spent the summer in Germany. Mom was working on her second book and doing research for it, and Dad was trying to get meetings with a bunch of companies his company wanted to work with. I was sent to drama camp, art camp, and outdoor adventure camp."

"You spent the summer away from your parents?"

"Obviously." 111 days, and this was where I was. I deserved it, I know, but still. Laurie was a big fucking weight to bear.

"Did you miss them?"

I shrugged. It was easier than saying it was more complicated than that, that missing someone means they have to actually be there, really there, for you to miss them.

"They sent postcards and stuff, and when they came to pick me up two days before school started, they said I'd grown a lot and showed me photos. The archive where Mom worked. The office building where Dad worked. The house they'd rented. The view from their kitchen window. They said they loved Germany so much they weren't sure they ever wanted to come home and laughed. I didn't."

"Why not?"

She knew damn well why I didn't—anyone with the slightest bit of a clue could know why—and so I ignored her and kept talking.

"I showed them the pictures I'd painted and gave them the video of the play I'd been in and—well, I didn't have anything to show from the outdoor adventure camp other than the certainty that I really didn't enjoy white-water rafting, climbing ropes, or forced marches that were called 'hiking.' They said the pictures were nice and watched the video while Mom worked on syllabi and Dad read through contracts. They both promised I wouldn't have to go to adventure camp again."

They never said they missed me, but I wasn't about to tell Laurie that.

When I looked at her, though, I could tell she already knew.

"And Julia?" was all she said, though.

"I started school, and it was the same as always. I just—I never said the right things fast enough or wore the right clothes soon enough. I never did things quite right."

Laurie nodded like she understood. "So you felt like you didn't belong?"

"No," I said, even though that was pretty much how I felt. I just hate it when Laurie talks like she knows me. "I had friends, Caro and Beth and Anne Alice, but we—well, we fought, like friends do, and I was always the first one to be talked about or laughed at or ignored. It was like no matter how hard I tried—that's probably it. I tried too hard. Nothing is worse than someone who wants something too much, you know?"

"Why?"

"Why do you think?" I said, and she clicked her goddamned pen. I wished Julia was there, because she'd have just gotten up, taken Laurie's pen, and thrown it out a window or something.

"So how did you meet Julia?" she said.

"She moved to Lawrenceville in October, and her first day at school was right before Halloween. She had to stand up in front of the whole class and talk about herself, and you could tell she wasn't nervous, that she wasn't afraid of anyone or anything. That was the first thing I noticed about her."

"What did she say?"

"I don't remember." But I did. She said she was twelve and that she'd been held back a year. She said it like it wasn't a big deal, like being held back was something we'd missed out on. And then, during recess, as I sat alone, banished from playing with Beth, Caro, and Anne Alice because Beth said I'd worn my hair wrong, she came up to me. She said, "I'm Julia. Want to go trick-or-treating with me on Halloween?"

And I did. How could I not? She was so cool, so

fearless, and she wanted to hang out with me? It was the best thing that had ever happened to me.

"But you became friends?"

I nodded. "Everyone wanted to be her friend, but I was her best friend." I still remember the first time she said that. Beth had just said, "Julia, you're totally my best friend," and Julia shrugged and said, "Amy's mine." The look on Beth's face was about the best thing ever. I still remember it.

"So you met, and you became friends." Truly, Laurie's ability to restate what I'd just said was a rare gift. And a fucking annoying one.

"Right," I said. "Like I just told you."

"What did you two do?"

"I spent a lot of time at her house. Her room was . . . it was great." The truth was, it was everything I wanted mine to be. She had a canopy bed and posters all over her walls. I could never get my posters to look right— they always got crooked, or curled up at the corners, so I always took them down.

Julia never even noticed stuff like that. If she wanted something on her wall she just stuck it up there, and the first time I went to her house she put in a CD and turned it up loud, sang and danced along with the music. She didn't tell me I was doing anything wrong when I joined in. She just said, "Isn't this fun?"

That's when I knew we would be friends forever.

"And her mother?" And there was Laurie circling in, hoping for whatever it is she hoped for during our sessions. She knew Julia's mother hated me. It was one of the first things I told her. She'd asked me if anything made me happy, and I'd said, "Julia's mother hates me for what happened. That makes me happy, because she should."

"Actually, her mom used to like me," I told Laurie now. "Hard to believe, right? But she did. For the first year Julia and I were friends, I think she hoped I'd somehow turn J into the kind of quiet loser I was before we met. I think Julia had gotten in trouble at her old school or something. I never really knew. Her mom never said, and Julia never talked about anything that happened before she moved to town. It was like before Lawrenceville she didn't exist."

"You never asked her about it?"

"No," I said. Why should I have? Whatever had brought Julia into my life was a good thing. An amazing thing.

"Did you like Julia's mother?"

What an odd question. But then, it was coming from Laurie. "Sure."

"But Julia fought with her."

"Yeah." I didn't add "And?" but Laurie must have sensed it because she just said, "You didn't fight with your own parents, right?"

Oh, please. "I didn't want Julia's mother to be my mother. We just got along for a little while."

"Then what happened?"

"Julia didn't start acting perfect."

Laurie nodded. "What did you do when you were at her house?"

"Regular stuff. Like, right after Thanksgiving that year, she had a slumber party, and everyone who was invited came. That's the way Julia was. People just wanted to be around her. We all stayed up talking for hours, but then, when everyone else had fallen asleep, Julia woke Caro up. We went out into the hall, and Julia told her off for all the things she and Beth and Anne Alice had done to me. She made Caro cry and I sort of felt bad for Caro, but not really because finally I wasn't the one crying."

"This is the same Caro you've mentioned before?"

I nodded, and Laurie scribbled something as I thought

83

about what happened after that. Caro had run off to the bathroom and we'd snuck downstairs and laughed about it. I felt so great. So free. We watched television for a while, and then Julia opened the cabinet where her mom kept her liquor and said, "What do you think?"

I can still remember the bottles. Brown, green, clear. We dared each other to try something. Julia had rum. I had vodka. It tasted awful, made my mouth and throat feel like they were on fire. But after a while my stomach felt warm, and then I felt warmer all over and everything seemed brighter. Better.

We ended up reading the best bits from her mom's stash of romance novels out loud to each other, laughing. It was so much fun. Right before we finally fell asleep Julia made me swear that since we'd be best friends forever and ever, we'd always tell each other everything. It was an easy promise to make. I couldn't imagine not telling her everything.

"When did you start drinking together?" Laurie said, and I looked her right in the eye and said, "I don't remember."

I knew what she'd do with that memory, how she'd twist it all around.

"Okay," Laurie said, and I could tell she knew I was lying. "Did you drink together a lot?"

"On the weekends, a little sometimes, when I'd stay over at her house and her mom was off trying to find Mr. Right. I'd stopped hanging out with Caro and Anne Alice and Beth, and it felt great, but for a while I worried that maybe Julia would decide she wouldn't want to be my friend."

I knew as soon as I'd said that I'd screwed up, because Laurie's interested expression was real. But she didn't say anything except, "Why did you drink?" which was such familiar territory that I wondered why she was going over it again.

"When I drank I had fun. I felt fun. When I drank, I didn't think about my parents signing off on my straight As report card with a quick 'great job' before heading off to yet another romantic dinner out. I didn't worry about being the only person who laughed at a joke some total loser made in class. I didn't worry about anything, and me and J would watch television and goof off."

What I didn't tell Laurie was when drinking changed for me.

The second semester of eighth grade, Julia got asked out by a ninth grader. He asked her to a party, and she said she'd go if I could come. She always did stuff like that for me. She always made sure I fit in.

I was really nervous about going, and when we got there I didn't know what to do. I felt totally out of place. I was the tallest person there, and even with my hair in a ponytail I still felt like it stuck out. Plus there were so many people and the music was so loud—it was totally overwhelming.

I followed Julia around until the guy she was with told me to get lost. I started to run off, feeling as small and stupid as Beth used to make me feel, but then Julia said, "Amy, wait," and told the guy to go to hell.

I couldn't believe it. He was a ninth grader! But she did. We went into the bathroom after that, and she pulled a bottle of peach schnapps out of her purse. She had some, I had some, and after a while we went back out to the party. And it was fun! I even sort of talked to a few people. J got her first hickey.

And then, amazingly enough, we—not just Julia, but both of us—got invited to another party. That time, I drank before we went and wasn't nervous at all.

"So drinking was fun?" Laurie said.

"I thought we were talking about Julia," I said, and I knew I sounded pissed off, but we were supposed to be talking about her. "And you know what? Julia was fun. She hated being bored. Before she got her license, we took the bus everywhere. And I mean everywhere. By the time she got her car, we already knew where everything remotely interesting in Lawrenceville and Millertown was. And when Julia started seriously hooking up with guys she never once dumped me to spend all her time with them. So many girls do that, you know? They hook up with someone a few times and drop everything because they think they're in love. Julia was like that, actually, always thinking she was in love, but no matter what, she never blew me off for someone else."

"Even for Kevin?"

Fucking Laurie. "Even with him."

"Do you think—?"

I cut her off before she could finish whatever stupid thing she was going to say. "When I ended up in the hospital six weeks before she . . . before she died, Julia was the first person I saw when I opened my eyes. She'd stayed with me the whole time, told everyone there she was my sister."

And when I'd woken up, and she'd told me that, she'd rested her head on my shoulder and said, "And really, you know, you are."

"You haven't ever said—" Laurie cleared her throat. "What about your parents? Were they there?"

"As much as they're ever anywhere," I said. "But Julia totally took care of them. They were all, 'What happened?' and when I reminded them that they could have taken three seconds to talk to the doctor, she said, 'Mr. and Mrs. Richards, let me tell you what really happened,' and when she was done with her story my mother was talking about some campus party she'd heard about, where this girl who drank a lot of what she thought was punch, but was actually mostly vodka, had to have her stomach pumped."

"Did she say anything else?"

"She told me she was glad I hadn't gotten as sick as that girl and to be more careful about taking drinks from strangers. And just so you won't ask, Dad nodded along with everything Mom said and asked me to promise that I'd be more aware."

Laurie scribbled stuff down, and I thought about how Julia had grinned at me after they left, walking off hand in hand like always to get coffee while they waited for me to be discharged, and said, "You know, they were really worried."

When I rolled my eyes she sat down next to me and said, "Really," and then we'd laughed over the story she'd told.

She'd said, "God, they're so much easier than my mom!" and she was right. Julia's mother would have cried and screamed and started in on J the second she woke up. She didn't trust Julia one bit, always wanted to know where she was going and who she'd be with. She'd question her over and over till Julia would yell, "Fine, whatever, I'm going," and leave.

"What happened after that?" Laurie said.

"Julia told the doctor she wasn't going anywhere when he came in to check on me and asked why she was still there. She scrounged up some old magazines and read the articles in funny voices. She bought me a candy bar when I said I wanted something to eat and the nurse I asked said, 'Honey, you'll just throw it up.' The nurse was right, but it didn't matter. Julia at least listened to me. No one else did. And when I was able to leave, she walked with me out to my parents' car, gave me a hug, and whispered, 'I'm going to call Kevin the second I get home and tell him we're never ever hanging out with that guy again. I really thought he was topping off your bottle but then, when you got so sick—I was scared, A.' My parents were there, sure. But Julia was really there. She always was."

And after all that, after I told Laurie about how Julia and I met and how amazing she was, this is what she said. This is what she wanted to know.

"How did you end up in the hospital?"

I stared at her. She'd said we were going to talk about Julia, and I had. And that was what she had to say? That? Hadn't she heard a word I said, hadn't she gotten how amazing Julia was?

She's such a crappy shrink.

"How did you end up in the hospital?" she asked again.

I sighed. "Drank too much. Remember, the thing you usually make me talk about?"

"I know," she said, and clicked her pen twice. "You said Julia told your parents what happened, that when she was done with her story they were relieved you were all right. What did she say?"

"That I thought I was drinking soda, but that someone had put a lot of liquor in it."

"And they believed this?"

I laughed. "Duh. It's my parents. Of course they did."

She clicked her pen again. "What really happened?"

"I just told you. Weren't you listening?"

"I'd like it if you'd elaborate a bit more. You did drink a lot, Amy, but this was the first and only time you ended up in the hospital because of it, right?"

I shrugged.

Laurie said, "I'd really like to know what happened," in a soft voice, like I wasn't talking because I didn't want to or couldn't. It was so annoying.

"Fine. Julia and I were hanging out with Kevin and this guy he sort of knew, okay? And when I went to the bathroom, the guy poured grain alcohol into my vodka."

"Why?"

"Um, because he was an asshole."

She clicked her pen.

"I don't really know why—I didn't ask him, you know, but it was probably because he got all pissed off when he tried to get me to go check out the bedrooms with him and I said 'no way.'"

"And so then—"

"Then I came back from the bathroom and drank. I didn't notice what he'd done until—well, I didn't notice. I passed out, and when Julia woke me up I started throwing up and couldn't stop. So she took me to the ER."

"I see. Was Julia with the boys when you went to the bathroom?"

"*Guys.* They weren't eleven. God. And yeah, she was. But she was, you know, busy with Kevin and didn't notice. If she'd noticed . . ."

"If she'd noticed, then what?"

"She would have said something."

"What if she did notice?"

"What?"

"Is it possible that she knew?"

"That's—you—" I couldn't even talk, I was so angry.

And what did Laurie do? More freaking pen clicking. "I'm sorry you're upset, but I'd like you to think about that night. What did you say before you went to the bathroom?"

"I don't remember," I said through clenched teeth.

But I did. I do. I was bored and not that drunk, had held back because I didn't like the guy who'd attached himself to me. He was someone Kevin knew a little, which meant absolutely nothing to me because I thought Kevin was a jerk. Plus he had mean eyes.

After telling him for the fourth time that no, I really didn't want to go check out the bedrooms with him, I told Julia I wanted to go home. She rolled her eyes but smiled and said, "Okay, fine, have another drink and we'll go."

"Fine," I said, and did my best to ignore Mean Eyes while I had a swig and then another. And then a few more. After a while, he put his hand on my thigh. I pushed it off and said I was going to the bathroom, knocking Julia's shoulder as I walked by, hoping she'd get the hint. When I got back Mean Eyes was gone and Julia said, "Got rid of him for you, A. So now ten more minutes is no problem, right?"

Before I could even answer she'd gone back to making out with Kevin. I went back to drinking, and after a while

I remember looking at the bottle and then at my hands and wondering why I could hardly move them when I hadn't had that much to drink. I told Julia I felt sort of sick, and after that it's all blank.

"You're sure you don't remember?" Laurie said.

"No," I said, and left. I didn't care if time was up or not. I just wanted to go.

I found Mom in the waiting room and told her we could leave. The receptionist asked if I wanted to schedule my next appointment.

I ignored her and said, "Come on, let's go," when Mom tried to walk over to her.

"Amy?" Mom said, looking surprised, and I said, "I can't come here anymore. I have to see someone else."

Mom frowned, and then asked the receptionist if she could talk to Laurie. She went back to her office. She was gone for a long time.

When she came back out her mouth was shaking the way it does when she's really upset.

"See?" I said, and she said, "We're not switching therapists, Amy."

I think she expected me to say something but I didn't. I didn't say a word the whole way home, and when we got there I went straight to my room. I had to be by myself. I had to let silence wash away Laurie and her stupid questions.

I hate that she said such dumb things. I hate her stupid office and her stupid pen clicking. I hate the chair she sits in and the stupid diplomas on her wall, and I really hate her stupid questions. I can't believe she asked me to talk about Julia and then didn't listen to a word I said.

TEN

WELL, I'VE HAD my very first date. Predictably, it was a total disaster.

Also, it wasn't a date at all.

I'd managed to block out the whole Mel thing—I mean, he didn't even know where I lived—so when the doorbell rang tonight and Dad answered it, calling out, "Amy?" in a weird voice, I figured—well, I thought maybe Julia's mother had come by.

I raced into the hallway. Julia's mother wasn't there, but Mel was. And so was Patrick. I stared at them. Mel waved and said, "Hey, ready to go to the movies?" Patrick looked at the floor.

"You're going out?" Dad said, his voice even weirder, and then Mom came in behind me and said, "Amy? What's going on?"

So then I had to ask my parents if I could go out on a date. In front of my date.

"But you didn't tell us about this before," Mom said at the same time Dad said, "Why didn't you mention this earlier?"

"Well, see . . ." I didn't know how to say, "Well, the thing is, I didn't mean to say yes, but apparently I did. Then I figured that since the guy didn't know where I lived there was no way he'd show up, and so I was ready for another Friday night at home. Which should be obvious since I'm wearing jeans and a shirt with a ketchup stain."

"I meant to," I finally said. "I just forgot."

"So now you want to go out with . . ." My father looked at Mel, who helpfully supplied his name again. "Who has brought along . . ." He looked at Patrick, who mumbled his name and leaned against the door like it was the only thing holding him up.

"Oh, right," Mel said cheerfully. "You're wondering about the whole bring-another-guy-along thing, aren't you?"

My father looked like he was having a stroke— not that Mel seemed to notice because he just kept talking. "Patrick needs a ride. No car, you know, and so I figured, hey, I can pick up some gas money." He laughed. No one else did, and now Patrick looked like he was trying to push himself inside the door and hide.

My parents really didn't seem impressed by any of this, and for one (very hopeful) second I thought they'd tell me, "No way," but then they shared a look, and although I think a little bit of it was probably related to some advice they'd gotten from reading Pinewood hand-outs or talking to Laurie, most of it was about them realizing if I went out they'd have the house to themselves for a while.

So they told me I could go. Dad did pull me aside before I left, though. He said, "Be home by eleven," which I didn't care about because, trust me, not a problem, and then, "Call us if you need anything. Anything at all," which I did care about because he looked like he really meant it, and he'd never said anything like that to me before.

My mind was racing as I walked out of the house. Why had Mel shown up? Wasn't he supposed to be walking with me or something instead of standing by his car tossing his keys from one hand to another and looking oddly proud of himself? What was Patrick doing here? Why hadn't I at least brushed my hair, or better yet, changed my shirt?

I was so busy trying to figure out what was going on that I—of course—walked right into Patrick.

What is it about him that makes me do stuff like that?

This time, though, walking into him wasn't my fault at all. He was standing in the middle of the driveway like he was stuck there but still, it was embarrassing.

"Sorry," we both muttered at the same time, and then I forgot all those questions I was asking myself. Why? Because Patrick's hand brushed against mine and something inside me twitched, shook itself awake. I stared at him and he stared at me, and suddenly my heart was pounding and my skin felt hot and flushed. I didn't like it at all.

"The front seat's kinda crowded," Mel said, and I swear, his voice actually startled me. For a second I'd forgotten he was there. I'd sort of—well, I'd sort of forgotten everything. Patrick looked pretty startled too, and we both looked away from each other. He stared at the ground. I looked at Mel's car. The front seat had a huge box sitting on the passenger side.

"Yeah, the box," Mel said. "My mom told me to drop it off for some charity thing she's doing, but I sort of forgot to. Would you mind sitting in the back with Pat—" He broke off and cleared his throat. I looked at him. He was looking at Patrick. They seemed to be having some sort of discussion without talking. It made me think of Julia, and that reminder of how they talked like she and I did, so easily in their own silent language, made my eyes prickle.

"I'll just sit in the back, and you can put the box next to me," I said because I knew what Mel was going to say and there was no way I was going to sit next to Patrick all the way to wherever we were dropping him off.

So we all got in the car, and there I was, in the back-seat with a box. Granted, I have very little dating experience (as in none) but this just didn't seem like normal date stuff. At all.

And then, as soon as we left my house, Mel started talking. First he asked how I was doing.

"Fine," I said.

"Good," Mel said, and cleared his throat again. Patrick looked out the window.

"What about you, Patrick?" Mel said, and Patrick muttered something too softly for me to hear.

"Well, man, then maybe I will make you pay me gas money," Mel said, and then sighed.

I knew then there was no way I was going to make it through whatever this was supposed to be, and started thinking about faking a stomachache as soon as we dropped Patrick off.

Except we didn't drop Patrick off.

Instead, we all went to the movies. As in me and Mel. And Patrick. So it definitely wasn't a date.

And then things got worse because when we got there, everyone in my freaking honors classes was there too. Someone called Mel's name and waved us over after we all got out of the car.

It was torture. Mel went and got tickets with most of the people, Patrick wandered off to stare at upcoming movie posters like they were the most interesting things he'd ever seen, and I got to stand there with Beth and her followers, including Corn Syrup.

Beth looked at me, said something about "social retards" just loud enough for me to hear, and then added, "Mel's just too nice, really."

I pretended I was deaf—I wished I was then, that's for sure—and then Beth dragged everyone into a discussion of whose butt was the biggest. ("Oh, mine is, totally." "No, mine is!" "No way, mine totally is!")

Mel came back with tickets, finally, and said, "Hey, you owe me ten for yours, okay?" as we got in line to get into the theater.

I dug around in my pockets, feeling for money that I knew wasn't there and vowing to never agree to anything Mel asked again, while Patrick stood next to Mel on his other side, hands jammed in his pockets and staring at the floor. Beth, who was right behind me, snorted and muttered something to Corn Syrup. I didn't think Mel heard her, but he must have because he muttered something to Patrick and then told me, "Never mind the money, I got it."

When we finally got into the theater Mel and I didn't even sit next to each other. I ended up in the seat next to the aisle one, Corn Syrup on one side of me and Patrick on the other. Patrick and I shared an armrest, but since neither of us was using it—I was sitting with my arms across my chest, feeling like I was back in middle school just waiting for Beth, Anne Alice, and Caro to decide they were mad at me for something, and Patrick was turned around in his seat, staring up the aisle at the door like he'd somehow forgotten where it was—there wasn't a problem.

Mel sat next to Caro, and they, naturally, started arguing over their armrest.

"I put my arm on it first," Caro said.

"No, you didn't, and besides, touching the armrest doesn't mean you own it," Mel said.

They ended up going at it just like they did in English class, and watching them, it became pretty clear that their arguing was a strange sort of flirting. They were even both doing that lean-in-toward-each-other thing when Beth, who was on Mel's other side, whispered something in his ear. Caro immediately tossed her hair and pretended to be bored with Mel. It didn't really work. She mostly looked unhappy.

Beth leaned back, bumping her arm into Mel's in a way that was more of a caress, and then whispered something else to him. He laughed, and I wondered why Mel wasn't dating her, but then the previews started and when Caro jumped during a trailer for a completely unscary horror movie I saw Mel reach one hand out toward her and then stop.

Now, as Beth so kindly pointed out, I may be a social retard, but even I could guess Mel liked Corn Syrup with that kind of clue. So how come he hadn't asked Caro to the movies? He didn't strike me as shy or anything.

And, more importantly, why had he brought me here?

By the time the movie started, I felt pretty bad, exhausted and sad and strange, and then something supposedly hilarious happened on-screen—some old guy stumbling around, crashing into things as he had a heart attack, landing with his hands grabbing the cute young girl's breasts right as he died—and everyone laughed. And there was something about that laughter, that *noise*— maybe it was all those voices in the dark, or maybe it was just that bits and pieces of all those laughs sounded like Julia's, like I could almost hear her. Whatever it was, the whole theater suddenly seemed like it wasn't real, and I was afraid if I moved everything around me would fall away and I'd be lost.

I felt shaky and weirdly dizzy—not like everything was spinning, but like I was spinning, and I knew it was wrong for me to be there. I shouldn't be at the movies, even if it was in the middle of a bizarre situation I didn't get and with a bunch of people I didn't like. I had to get out. I had to get away and—

Drink.

I wanted a drink. I wanted one so bad.

Somehow I managed to get out of the theater, and as I was wiping my sweaty hands on my jeans and heading to the lobby, I realized I hadn't had to step over anyone in order to leave. Patrick had left too.

I thought it was weird, but then Patrick was weird, and then I couldn't think at all because the unsteadiness came back, the lobby and the crowds of people standing around waiting for their movie to start turning into a spinning blur of color and faces. I had to get out of there. Even more than I wanted a drink, I wanted to go home.

I thought about going back and telling Mel I was leaving, but I figured he wouldn't even notice I was gone and I was starting to feel like I was going to pass out or worse. I managed to find a pay phone—Mom and Dad want me to prove I'm "ready" to have a cell again, which is stupid because who would I call if I had one?—and called home. Dad said he'd come get me right away and as soon as I hung up I sat down on the floor right by the phone, not caring that people were staring.

That didn't last long. I've always hated it when people stare at me, because I know they're seeing how I'm too tall and have weird-colored hair, and being the only person sitting down in a huge shifting swarm of people meant everyone was stepping on my feet or stepping over them and staring at me, the girl on the floor. I stood up and scuttled along the wall to an exit.

Outside, I felt better. Everything didn't seem so bright, so closed in, and I rubbed my still sweating and now shaking hands down my arms. A couple pushed past me, bumping into me like I wasn't there. Maybe I wasn't.

I sure felt like I wasn't. I walked blindly down the sidewalk, head bent so I wouldn't have to see anything, and hoped Dad would come soon.

"The sidewalk pretty much ends here," someone said.

It was Patrick. He was sitting down, leaning against the theater wall, almost hidden from the enormous lights that were shining down on everything, including the parking lot.

"Sorry," I muttered. My voice sounded strange, far away. I looked back at the lobby. It looked even brighter and more crowded than before, cartoon fake. No way could I ever go back. I wanted to be somewhere, anywhere else. I wanted to feel better. I wanted a drink again. I hated myself for it, but I did.

"You should sit down," he said. I looked at him. He wasn't looking at me. He was staring straight ahead with his arms folded tight around his bent knees. Everything went blurry then, and when my vision cleared it was too clear, like the world had turned into nothing but sharp edges waiting to cut me open.

I sat down. I had to, or I was afraid I'd fall down. I knew I was having a panic attack. I'd had them after . . . after what happened. After Julia died, and all through my first few weeks in Pinewood. I hadn't had one in a while, though, and I'd forgotten how they made everything seem like it—and I—was going to fall apart. How they reminded me of how trapped I was.

I tried to stare straight ahead like Patrick, but the world still looked odd. Wrong. I stared down at the ground and tried to talk to myself the way Laurie taught me to. I told myself it was just panic, that I was upset, on edge, and that it would pass.

It didn't work. I felt worse; less connected to myself, to everything. My hands shook, and I could feel my heart beating too fast, racing and skipping beats, and I couldn't close my eyes because when I did all I saw was Julia leaning against me, crying as we walked toward a waiting car.

"Is this the first time you've gone out since J—"

"Yes," I said, and started to stand up. I didn't want to move, didn't want to go back to the lobby, but I didn't want to talk about me and Julia.

"I'm sorry about earlier," Patrick said. "Showing up with Mel and everything, I mean. It was—you know."

I didn't but nodded anyway.

"There was a carnival just down the road," Patrick said. "Two years ago." His voice sounded funny, thin and stretched out. I figured he was high. Strangely, it made me feel better. High guys were easy to deal with.

"Sure, I remember," I said, even though I didn't.

Patrick looked at me.

"No, you don't," he said, and he wasn't high at all. I could see it in his eyes, bright and clear and in pain, and suddenly I did remember the carnival. I remembered it coming to town, setting up in the parking lot of a closed discount store. I remembered what happened there.

No wonder Patrick had left the movie.

"How's your dad?"

Patrick shrugged. "The same." Two years ago, when Patrick had just moved to town and was a new star at school, super smart and an athlete all the jocks, even the seniors, were talking about, his dad had a stroke at the carnival. He'd almost died. I'd forgotten all about it.

"People forget stuff like that," Patrick said, and in his eyes I could see he knew exactly what I'd been thinking. What I'd just remembered. "Stuff that . . . something happens that changes your whole life, and people tell you how sorry they are and all that, but then, after a while, it's like you're the only one who remembers. It'll happen to you too. People will forget what happened to Julia. They'll forget her."

"I won't."

"No," he said. "You won't. Even if you want to forget, you'll remember. I can still see my dad's face. He was mad about how much it cost to get in, kept talking about it. People were staring. I wasn't listening, wanted to go find my friends, and then he sort of . . . he just gave me this look. This weird look, like he didn't know me, like he didn't know anything, and then he was on the ground . . ." Patrick stopped talking. He looked like he was back there, like he was trapped in one horrible moment. I know what that feels like.

"The movie made you think about it, didn't it?"

He laughed, and I was sorry I'd said anything because his laugh didn't sound like a laugh at all. It sounded like pain.

"Everything makes me think about it. I know it shouldn't. He didn't die. He's still alive; he's doing okay, learning how to walk again and stuff, so really, I'm pretty damn lucky. I shouldn't be so . . . I shouldn't be out here, hiding. I should be okay."

"I didn't say—"

"You didn't have to. It's the truth." He wrapped his arms around his legs again. "Do you miss the person you were before she died?"

"I . . . No." I did, though. I do. I thought things were hard before but they weren't. I never knew how lucky I was until it was too late.

He looked at me again. He didn't say anything but his eyes were easy to read. In them I saw he was calling me a liar without ever saying a word. Laurie would love him.

"It wouldn't matter if I did," I said sharply. "It's not like I can go back."

"If you could, though? If you could go back and change things a little, make it so Julia would live, would—?"

"You can't say things like that. You shouldn't . . . you can't think like that." I stood up, shaking. "I don't think like that."

"Amy?"

It was Dad. I looked behind me and saw him standing a few feet away, on the lit part of the sidewalk. He looked worried.

I forced myself to smile. His expression relaxed a little, and I knew Patrick was right about one thing. Everyone needed me to be okay.

"You're right," Patrick said as I walked away. He was talking quietly but I heard him. "You can't go back. No matter how much you want to, you never can."

I didn't answer him. I didn't look back. I walked over to Dad and followed him to the car. When I got in I fiddled with the radio so I could have something to do. So I could pull myself together. I told Dad Patrick was no one when he asked, said he was just a guy in one of my classes who'd asked about homework while I was waiting for Dad to come get me. I said, "No, I'm fine, I'm just not ready to go out yet," when Dad asked me if I was okay. I said, "I promise, I would tell you if something was bothering me," when he asked again.

I could see Patrick in the side mirror as we drove away. He was looking at me. He was just a shadow, dark against dark, but I saw him.

114 days

Julia, you—

You knew.

It's 4:00 a.m., and I'm sitting on the bathroom floor. It took me forever to fall asleep because everything Patrick said was rolling around in my head, but I did. I fell asleep and woke up shaking from a dream that wasn't one, from the memory of your open eyes staring unseeing into mine.

I'm sorry for what I did, and you know that, right? You have to know that. But J, did you—

You knew, didn't you?

That night, the one where you didn't want to leave Kevin at that party, you knew what that guy did. I know what you said at the hospital really meant now, J. Why didn't you say anything that night? Why?

No.

You didn't know.

You couldn't have known. You were wrapped up in Kevin, desperate to be with him, but you were going to take me home. You said you would. You got rid of that guy for me. You might have seen something, but it wasn't enough to make you sure of anything, and if you had, you would have said something.

You didn't know.

Right?

I hate Laurie for this. I want my memory of waking up and seeing you in the hospital unchanged. I don't want to think there was a shadow in your eyes. I don't want to think that when you hugged me before I went home and said you were scared, you meant something else. I don't want to think you meant you were sorry.

But, Julia, I know you, and "sorry" was a word you were never able to say. Did you—is that what you were trying to say?

I don't want to think about this anymore.

ELEVEN

I DIDN'T EVEN MAKE IT to school today.

Well, I did, but only for a little while.

I was pretty tired when I got there this morning. I haven't been sleeping that well, not since—well, not since I wrote to Julia after Friday night.

I know Julia didn't know exactly what that guy did, but it just . . . it's there, in my head, and it won't go away.

At school, I forgot to take the long way to my locker and ended up passing hers. I tried not to notice it, but of course I did. I hate what they've done to it so much.

Mel walked by as I was opening my locker. I pretended I didn't see him, but he slowed down and said, "Hey, Amy." He was with Patrick, who was (as usual) staring at the floor. When I looked over at them Mel waved and then nudged Patrick, who looked up from his inspection of the floor long enough to briefly meet my eyes.

When he did, I thought of all the stuff he'd said at the movies. I thought about what I'd realized afterward. My heart started thumping fast, beating so hard I could feel it. My locker looked like it was really far away even though I had one hand resting on it, and I knew I had to leave school. I wasn't ready for it. I had to get away, go somewhere and just . . . shut off my brain or something. I could go home, lie in bed with the covers pulled up over my head.

I could go home and scrounge up some money, then go out and find something to drink. I knew all the places Julia went to get stuff for me. I could do it on my own.

After all, hadn't I made it so that's how things had to be?

I shut my locker, slamming it closed with one fist, and headed toward the exit at the end of the hall. Giggles was standing there, mouth puckered like she'd had two lemons shoved in it, nodding at something a teacher was saying and glaring at anyone who tried to get near the door. I turned back around and ducked into the bathroom, figuring Giggles would toddle off when the bell rang. Once the bell rang I could leave.

Once the bell rang I had to leave.

I passed Mel again on my way to the bathroom. He said something to me. I nodded like I'd heard him. I didn't, though. The only thing I wanted to hear was the bell.

The bathroom was empty. Giggles must have passed through earlier and cleared everyone out. I tapped a fist—I couldn't seem to unknot my fingers—against the paper towel dispenser and hoped the bell would ring soon. The door slammed open and Caro came in. She looked like she was trying to look bored, but instead she just looked upset.

"Mel asked me to come in here to see if you were okay."

I ignored her.

"Fine, I'm going. I'm sure he'll be in here in thirty seconds anyway. And just so you know, ignoring him apologizing for Friday to make him feel bad isn't going to make him like you or anything. He's just being nice because he's, well, Mel. Everyone else knows exactly who—and what—you are."

I looked at her. She should have looked angry. What she said sure was angry. And she did look a little pissed off. Mostly, though, she looked anxious.

She was glancing around like Beth might be lurking in the corner, waiting to get mad because what she'd just said hadn't been preapproved. It was so stupid. She was so stupid. She was afraid to be angry without Beth's permission.

I walked over to her and watched her look around anxiously again. Such a stupid sheep. "He doesn't like me, you moron. He likes you, and if you'd get your head out of your ass for five seconds you'd realize that, and then the two of you could stop acting like you're in some crap romantic comedy where you have to argue before you get together and just do it already."

Her mouth fell open, and her eyes got all watery, but she didn't say a word. I pushed past her, the damn bell finally ringing as I headed into the hall and then out of school.

I couldn't believe what I'd just said. I never said stuff like that. Julia said stuff like that, and I wished I could. It didn't feel as great as I thought it would, but at least I wasn't going to have to deal with anyone for a while.

A while turned out to be maybe two minutes. I didn't even make it off the school grounds. I didn't even make it to the stupid planters by the parking lot before Caro grabbed my arm—hard—and yanked me around to face her.

"I really hate you," she said, or at least I think she did. It was hard to tell because she was crying.

I pulled away from her and kept walking, crossing the parking lot and finally leaving school. Corn Syrup's feelings were hurt? Boo-hoo. I was so going to go home, find some money, and then find a drink. Or many drinks.

The weird thing was, I kept hearing her cry. Even when I was cutting through the neighborhood that's full of old people and little yappy dogs, I could still hear her.

I turned around after I passed an old guy who almost backed into me with his big-ass car, and she was walking behind me, still crying. I stopped walking. She did too. We just sort of stared at each other, and I guess the look on my face must have been something because she stopped crying long enough to say, "Look, I don't know what I'm doing here, okay?"

She sounded so miserable, so lost, that all the stuff about Julia and everything else that was clawing inside me, scratching me raw and making me desperate for a drink—it stilled. Because what she said and how she said it . . . it was how I felt too. How I always feel.

I don't know why I'm here either, except that it's what I deserve and that—I know it's right, but I'm so lost without Julia. So lonely.

I guess maybe that's why I ended up going to Caro's house. She didn't ask me, exactly, just said, "I'm going home. If you want to . . ."

We walked there in silence. I remembered her living all the way at the edge of town but apparently she moved and now lives about ten blocks from the high school. I hadn't known that, but then I never thought about Caro after me and Julia became friends, except for the occasional middle school flashback when I was nervous, and in those, Caro was always the shadow behind Beth, her little puppet.

I thought things hadn't changed much, but Caro is different now. Sort of. For instance, the whole . . . whatever thing at school.

And then, when we got to her house, I found out she's a vegetarian too.

"You want something to eat?" she said when we walked in. "I don't do meat, but my parents do if you want a sandwich or something."

"Oh," I said. "I don't—I don't eat meat either."

"Cheese?"

"What?" I said, and she grinned, just a little.

"Do you eat cheese?"

I nodded, and we ended up making grilled cheese sandwiches and eating them while we watched TV. It should have been weird, the whole sandwich thing (plus the being-at-her-house thing) but it wasn't. It didn't feel normal, but it felt okay. And it definitely felt a lot better than being at school.

I was almost done with my sandwich when she cleared her throat and said, "You know, I wish I was tall, like you."

I faked a smile while I ate my last crust and flashbacked to her and Beth and Anne Alice calling me "skyscraper" in fourth grade, but she said, "No, Amy, seriously. I would love it."

"Yeah, it's a joy trying to find jeans and having the legs end around your shins. Or knees."

"But you totally stand out. Even when we were kids you did. People would always talk about how tall you were, like a model, and how pretty your hair was and—"

"I don't remember that."

"Come on. Remember when we went to the aquarium and everyone we saw kept saying you had beautiful hair?"

"All I remember is the bus ride home." Stuff being rubbed in my hair, giggles filling my ears. It was so hard not to cry, but I didn't. I wouldn't let myself. I just sat there and hoped it would be over soon.

I was sure she'd be all "What do you mean?" about it but she muttered, "Yeah," and then said, "You just sat there. If you'd just turned around and said something, anything, then maybe—"

"Beth would have told everyone to put more crap in my hair?"

"No, I would have . . . yeah, okay. She would have said that, and we would have done it. Beth was—she is—"

"A bitch?"

"Yeah," Caro said, and then looked horrified. "I mean—she's not, not really. She's my best friend and . . ." She sighed. "Who am I kidding? She's a total bitch. She knows I like Mel—how, I don't know, because I didn't tell her. But it doesn't matter. She's decided she likes him, and Beth always gets what she wants."

"Not always," I said, but I was lying. Girls like Beth do always get what they want. It's like an unwritten law or something. And I could tell from the way Caro was looking at me that she knew I was lying too.

"I keep hoping she'll get bored and go after someone else," she said. "Dating Mel means hanging out with Patrick, and she really doesn't like him. He's so . . . well, he's so quiet, it's kind of freaky."

"Because he's quiet?"

"He's not ordinary quiet, you know? He's just . . . always quiet. Didn't you see him disappear at the movies on Friday? Or maybe you'd already left before he did?"

When I didn't say anything she shrugged. "Anyway, after his dad's stroke he had to help out because his parents are pretty old, and he ended up missing a lot of school. He made it all up, or whatever, but I guess what happened to his dad messed him up because when he came back he just . . . he wasn't the same."

"How?" I couldn't help it. I had to know.

"He didn't talk to his friends. He didn't talk to anyone, and I think if Mel hadn't just assumed that when he talked, Patrick would talk back, he might never have spoken to anyone again. It's like just being there is difficult for him, and not because it's school and we're all sick of it. I think something about being around a lot of people—or anyone, really—bothers him. Weird, huh?"

"His dad had a stroke at a carnival, remember? Lots of people around."

"Right, I forgot. That makes sense. I guess it explains why he left the movie too. There was that thing at the beginning, with the old guy . . ."

"I remember," I said, and thought about Patrick sitting outside the movie theater. Where he was sitting. How he was sitting. What he said. How he knew exactly what it was like to be a totally different person even though you looked exactly the same.

"It's too bad, you know?" Caro said. "What happened to him, I mean. He was totally someone once. He did stuff. But now he doesn't do anything. I couldn't believe he was at the movies, actually. Mel must have dragged him there."

"Maybe," I said, even though I was sure he had.

"I've seen Patrick at two parties, maybe, in the past couple of years, and he always leaves after, like, ten minutes and goes and waits for Mel to drive him home. It's just so sad how some people totally get messed up when someone . . ." She trailed off. "Not that you're . . . I mean, everyone's messed up, aren't they?"

I made an agreeing noise and tried to remember if there was a crosstown bus stop nearby. Corn Syrup attempting to do deep? I definitely didn't need that.

"I mean, look at me," she continued. "I'm afraid to talk to a guy I really like because my best friend, who I hate to the point where I imagine her getting hit by a car at least twice at day, has decided she might want him."

"Well, you could—never mind." I got up. Bus stop or no bus stop, I was out of there. The last thing I needed to do was hang around and point out the obvious.

"What?"

I sighed, because really, for a supposedly smart person, she sure was dumb. "Beth treats you like crap, right?"

Caro shrugged.

"So stop hanging out with her."

"Oh, right. Great idea, because high school is totally the best place to do something that will make sure I have absolutely no friends."

I hadn't known Caro could do sarcasm. I sat back down.

"You know, it was easy for you to ditch Beth, but then you had Julia. I've never had someone like that, who would stand up for me no matter what. You were so lucky, Amy."

Were. Past tense. I stood back up. "Look, I gotta—"

"I hated her, you know. Ever since that party when we were in sixth grade—"

"Yeah, so sorry you got called on your shit."

"Like I was the only one doing stuff to you," Caro said quietly. "But that's not even it. You basically stopped talking to me after you met her. You just—you acted like we'd never been friends."

"We were never friends. You and Beth and Anne Alice were friends."

"Beth and Anne Alice were friends. Do you know how awful my life would be if Anne Alice hadn't moved to Los Angeles two years ago? They treated me just like you, Amy, only I had to deal with it for a hell of a lot longer.

Don't you remember what they did to me at my tenth birthday party? Or how about the time in fourth grade when you, Anne Alice, and Beth formed a secret club when I was out with chicken pox?"

"Nope." I hadn't remembered, anyway, until she said it. And then I did. I remembered Beth and Anne Alice showing up in matching sweaters at Caro's birthday party and talking about what a great sleepover they'd had while Caro unwrapped her gifts.

I remembered that stupid club and how excited I was to be in it. I totally ignored all the notes Caro sent when she got back asking for a hint about the club name and begging me to talk to Beth and Anne Alice for her. Instead, I laughed with them about how badly she wanted to get in.

"Of course you don't remember. I mean, why should you care that the last conversation I had with a real friend was about Chester, and how he was really sick and I was afraid he was going to die? Your coat's over on that chair, by the way, and the bus stop is two blocks over."

I stopped walking across the room. "What do you want me to say, Caro? I'm sorry I wasn't more help when we discussed your sick dog. I was eleven. I didn't have a degree in grief counseling."

"God, you are so stupid. It's not what you said, Amy. It's the fact that the last time I talked to someone I could really call a friend was when I was eleven years old."

"Oh."

Caro rolled her eyes at me and got up, grabbed my jacket, and shoved it at me. "Here."

"Look, I'm—I just—" I looked at Caro, who was staring back at me, her mouth a thin angry line. "You never said anything to me."

"Oh, I'm sorry. I guess after you and Julia told me off I should have come up to you and said, 'Hey, Amy, I totally miss hanging out with you.' Please. You and Julia would have made me cry again and loved it."

"We wouldn't have . . ." I trailed off. We totally would have. "You just—you always seemed happy. You still do, mostly."

Caro twirled a piece of hair around one finger and smiled a huge, happy smile. Even her eyes shone bright. Her voice, however, was a different story. It was flat. Drained. "I've had a lot of practice. See you around, Amy."

I was glad to get out of there—big-time glad—but as I walked to the bus stop I kept thinking about what she'd said. The last time she felt like she'd really talked to someone was when she talked to me about Chester? The last real friend she thought she had was me?

Was that why she'd come after me this morning? Did she—was today about her trying to be friends with me?

I laughed out loud then because come on, really. And then I tried to picture Caro saying anything she'd said to me to Beth. I couldn't do it. The most I'd ever heard her say to Beth was, "You look totally amazing!" or "You are *so* right!"

I walked back to Caro's house. Her eyes were red when she opened the door. "Oh," she said, and then, "What?"

"So what happened?"

"What?"

"To Chester."

"He died."

"Oh. I'm sorry. He was a nice dog." God, I sounded like such an idiot. An idiot who should just leave and go back to the bus stop already.

"He was a great dog," Caro said when I was halfway down her front steps. "Jane took a picture of him the night before he died. She saved it forever, and last year, she did this mosaic thing with it, like a hundred tiny pictures made into one big picture, and won first place in a photography show."

I turned around. "Jane's a photographer? Jane?" Caro's sister was never able to take pictures. When Caro and I were eight, we went to the Millertown Festival with her family and Jane was allowed to take all the pictures. Every single one of them came out blurry, or were of things like the edge of someone's knee or the top of someone's head and a whole lot of clouds.

"I know." Caro laughed. "You should have seen Dad when she told him she was changing her major from business to visual arts. But she's pretty good. She took an amazing picture of Mom over the summer. You want to see it?"

So I went back inside and saw the photo—it was actually pretty good—and Caro and I ended up talking. Not about school or Beth, but other stuff. I found out her mom had a blocked blood vessel in her brain last spring, and had to have emergency surgery.

In the photo Jane took, Caro's mom was outside, sitting in the sun and smiling at the camera, the top of her head totally wrapped in bandages. Caro told me every time her mom gets a headache she worries something bad will happen.

"Stupid, right?" she said.

"No," I said, and then I ended up telling her about Pinewood.

I don't know why I did. I just felt like it, I guess. I didn't even feel weird. Well, maybe a little. But she wasn't— she didn't react like I thought she would. She didn't say anything stupid, and she didn't try to be all positive or sympathetic or anything. She just said, "What was it like?"

"I don't know," I said. "Like how those places are, I guess. Lots of talking and stuff. Oh, and every day I had to 'participate in active movement.'"

"Like dancing?"

"No, it was just a fancy name for gym class," I said, and she smiled.

"So gym and talking."

"And bad food," I said. "I mean, I like salads and stuff, but you try sixty days with no junk food. It's not normal."

"No junk food at all?"

"None."

"Ugh," she said, and went into the kitchen, came back with a box of those super expensive chocolate-covered ice cream bars. "I was saving these for when I study for the next physics test, but you totally need one."

I had one and wow, did I forget how great ice cream is. I never meant to eat it again, because it was something Julia and I had done together, but it just looked so good. And Caro isn't—she's not like I remembered. She's human, for one thing. She's also kind of fun. I didn't know anyone besides Julia could be fun.

116 days

J,

Forget what I said before . . . you know, about what happened. Promise you'll forget it, okay? Because I'm—things have been weird lately. Like today, for instance.

Today, I ended up spending the day with Corn Syrup (don't be mad, okay?) and missed school.

I also got home late. (You remember how crappy the crosstown bus is.) I got home so late, in fact, that Mom and Dad actually noticed. I didn't even get a chance to open the front door because they marched right out as soon as I came up to the house.

It was like something out of a television show, the way they started firing questions at me. "Are you okay?" "Why did you miss school?" "Have you been drinking?"

"Yes." "I don't know." "No."

"Where were you?" "What were you thinking?"

"Nowhere special. And I just . . . I don't know."

"Nowhere special? And you don't know what you were thinking when you skipped school? Nothing comes to mind at all?" That was Dad, his voice rising with every word.

"Amy, these aren't answers." That was Mom. She was holding Dad's hand. I could see their fingers laced white tight against each other.

I didn't want to talk about Corn Syrup. My parents would think it meant Caro and I were going to be friends, and I wasn't up for explaining how high school really worked. You know how it is . . . but then you aren't here.

"Look," I told them. "I just wandered around. I needed to think."

My mother started to say something else and then stopped, looking lost and upset. Dad ran a hand through his thinning hair, which is a paler shade of my own. He looked angry and lost too.

"I don't know what to say to you," he finally said, his voice cracking, and he and Mom just stood there, looking at me.

It was so . . . it was amazing, seeing them like that, wild-eyed and upset over me (me!) but at the same time it made me think of you and your mother. It made me think of that night, of standing in the hospital staring at the police officers talking to me. Their faces came at me in pieces. Forehead, nose, chin, voices. Their voices sounded so far away.

Then I heard your mother. All she said was your name but it sounded torn out of her. JuliaJuliaJulia. *Julia!*

I wanted a drink again. I wanted to forget today, the past few months, who I am now. I didn't want this, all of us standing around outside acting out scenes from a play none of us knew the lines to.

I told them all of that, J. Every single word. The play bit was the best. Mom actually flinched. I liked that. I liked that they were upset. Now I know why you said things that would make your mom's voice rise furiously and her face turn red. I know why you did it with a little smile on your face.

You owned her when she was like that. You were all she could see.

I pushed past them like they weren't there, like all those years where they looked past me to see each other, and went inside. They followed me, and when I glanced back over my shoulder I saw them looking at me. I watched them search my face like it held answers to everything.

Finally, I had what I wanted from them. Finally, they were really looking at me. But what it took to get that . . . I turned away and went upstairs.

The thing is—and you know this—is that my parents were never cut out to be parents. I mean, they're not the kind of parents you think of when someone says something like that, people who specialize in dark closets and hard slaps, creating children who know the only way they'd be safe is if they were never born.

My parents just didn't plan on having kids. I know that's not that big a deal. So they didn't want kids. I'm not the first mistake ever born.

And look, I know I'm lucky. I live in a nice house in a nice neighborhood. I live with two parents who are still married to each other. Who still love each other. I've never been spanked, never been called names or insulted. They've never even yelled at me.

And that's just it. I was never even worth the effort of a raised voice. I know it's sick, bitching because my parents never yelled at me. Oh poor me, being able to do whatever I wanted. You always said I had it made, that my parents were cool. You liked them. You liked the way they always said, "Oh, hello, Julia," when you came over and never asked where we were going or when we would be back. You said it was a lot better than your mom, who always asked about your clothes and your hair and your friends, endless questions.

I envied you.

Oh, my parents made room for me. They gave me birthday parties when I was young enough to want them and came to my school plays and sometimes took me with them on vacation. I always got an allowance and great presents on the holidays and my birthday. I got hugs if I asked for them and always a good-night kiss on the cheek. But that was it. I was there. They knew it. The end. They'd filled their hearts up with each other and didn't need anything else. They didn't need anyone else.

And when I stopped trying to please them by being as perfect as I could be, when I stopped getting all As and stopped participating in all the worthless after school activities I was in, they said they understood. They said sure, I could move into the attic when I asked. They said bye, have a nice time when I'd yell that you and I were going out. They said hey, it's okay, not everyone is cut out for advanced classes when my grades dropped to average or just below. They said they knew being a teenager was rough.

They never asked how I was.

TWELVE

I TAKE BACK EVERYTHING I told Julia about my parents before. I was lucky then, back when they left me alone. When Julia was around.

Mom and Dad came upstairs after dinner—which I refused to go down for, not just because I didn't want to deal with them, but because I also wanted to think about the hanging-out-with-Caro thing—and sat on my bed.

They said (predictably, at the same time), "We'd like to talk to you about Julia."

I ignored them and stared at my bedspread.

"We're not leaving," Dad said, and the way he said it should have told me what was coming. "Your mother and I feel that your behavior today—and not just that, but all of your behavior lately—has been about what happened to Julia, and we want you to tell us about the night she—"

"You were at the hospital, remember? You saw me come in. You probably saw them bring her . . . her body in, and I don't know what more there is to say."

"We'd like you to talk to us," Mom said. "Tell us exactly what happened. How it made you feel. We . . . honey, we want you to know you can always talk to us."

"I can talk to you," I said, echoing them, and they both nodded.

Now I could talk and they would listen. Now they wanted to. Now. It made something twist hard inside me because I always wanted them to really talk to me, really listen to me, but if I'd known what would make it happen—God, if I'd only known . . .

"Please, Amy," Dad said. "Your mother and I think this would be helpful for all of us. We haven't pressed you, but we think you need to talk about it. It would help us help you."

Something bitter rolled through me then. They wanted to help me now, when it was too late, when nothing could be done. I looked at their faces, so eager to be "the parents" when before they just wanted to be "Colin and Grace, who happen to have a daughter."

"I killed her."

Silence. Not comfortable silence. Shocked silence. There's a difference. Shocked silence hangs heavy, presses down on you.

"But you weren't—you weren't driving the car," Mom said, leaning in and putting a hand on my knee. "Julia was driving."

I moved away. "I told her we should leave, I walked her to the car, I told her to get in. I told her to put on her seat belt. I told her to drive."

"Amy," Dad said. "That doesn't mean—"

"It does," I said. "It does because I made sure she wanted to leave. I wanted—I wanted us to, and we did, and then she . . ."

And then I killed Julia.

I told them how I did it. I told them because I could see they didn't believe me.

I knew, once I told them, that they would.

"We went to a party," I said. "Julia's boyfriend, Kevin, was supposed to be there. I went in first, because Julia wanted me to make sure he was there, and I saw him leading some freshman girl upstairs."

I'd known it was coming, I knew how Kevin was. I knew Julia loved him, but he . . . he kept messing around with other girls, and she'd get mad and yell and say she'd never see him again.

But she always did. Why? I still don't get that. She said she loved him, but, really, what good is love?

What does it do? Julia loved Kevin, and he hurt her, and I wanted her to see that. I wanted her to understand that she could do better.

Mom and Dad were looking at me. Not confused, exactly, more like . . . more like they thought they were safe.

They were wrong.

"I made sure Kevin had time to do what I knew he would," I said, making sure I spoke slowly even as the words stung my mouth, curdled my heart. "I went and found Julia. I told her he wasn't there, but that I'd heard he would be. So we waited."

We waited, me drinking in the car while Julia tapped her fingers against the steering wheel and sang along to a love song, shaking her head when I offered her the bottle.

"After I got drunk," I said, "I told her we should go in. And when we did, and she couldn't find Kevin, I said I'd heard some girls talking about him going upstairs."

He was upstairs, and he was with another girl, just like I knew he would be, and I waited for Julia to finally be through with him. To realize he wasn't going to change, toss off a few words that would turn him into nothing, slam the door, and move on.

But that's not what happened. She saw everything and started to cry. I didn't want her to cry. I wanted to help her. I wanted her to be free of Kevin, free of what she called love. I thought that if we left she'd feel better.

"So you told her that her boyfriend was upstairs, and you knew he was?" Mom said. "Amy—"

"I knew he'd be fucking someone else," I told her, and wondered if the look on my face was as horrible as the way I knew my heart was, ruined and bitter and wrong. "I knew Julia would go up and see it. And that's what happened. I did that. I made it happen. And when she got upset like I knew she would, I told her we should go."

Let's go, everything will be fine, school's finally over and summer's here. Screw Kevin and his freshman skank, you can do better and you will. It'll be okay. We just need to get out of here.

I just wanted her to stop crying. I wanted her to be happy. I didn't . . . I didn't want to think about the fact that I'd made sure she'd seen her boyfriend cheating on her again.

I didn't want to think about how I'd hurt her.

I didn't realize I'd hurt her even more.

"So you—?" Dad said, and his voice cracked a little.

"Yes," I said. "I was the reason we left the party. I made it so we had to. And when we did leave, I had to tell her to get in the car twice because she was crying so hard. I told her to put on her seat belt, and then I buckled it for her. I had to—I even had to tell her to start the car."

I could tell Mom was getting ready to say something, so I kept talking. "I told Julia to drive. She did and I didn't care where we were going, only that I'd gotten her out of there. We were going fast, so fast it was like flying. . . ." My throat felt tight and sticky. I looked over at Mom and Dad. They were still looking at me.

I could change that.

"Then the car—we went around a corner and spun out," I said. "It happened so fast. There was so much noise, this weird ripping screech, and then it was like—then it was like we were flying for real. I could feel it. Everything was so quiet and the car was going round and round. I could see the sky. I still remember seeing all the stars turn. Then my head hit the window and I passed out. And Julia . . ." My voice trailed off, broken.

"Amy," Dad said. He was holding my hand. I hadn't even noticed him taking it. I pulled away so I wouldn't have to feel him drop it.

"When I woke up everything looked so strange. The ground was up in the sky, and the road was where the stars should be. I tried to look around and a branch hit my face. We were . . . the car had flipped, been thrown up into the sky, and we were caught in a bunch of trees. There were huge holes in the windshield, places where it had broken when branches pushed through, and I . . . I saw her. I saw what I'd done to her."

Mom started to cry. I wanted to stop talking then but I couldn't. It just kept coming out.

"I looked at Julia," I said. "She—she was so quiet. I said her name but she didn't answer. She was . . ." I wanted to close my eyes, but I knew what I'd see if I did.

"She was looking at me. There was—she'd put this glitter stuff on her face and it had rubbed off, smudged around her eyes. I told her that because I knew she'd want to fix it and she didn't—she didn't move. She just kept looking at me. Her eyes were—they were wide-open but she didn't see me."

Mom started crying harder. Dad was crying too. I stopped talking. We sat there and they cried. I watched them. My eyes were totally dry.

Mom wiped at her eyes and reached for me. "You look so upset."

"All those years of paying attention to me are really paying off, huh?" I said, and pushed her hands away. She looked like I'd hit her. She started crying again. After a while she stopped. I rolled away and stared at the wall until she and Dad got up.

"It's okay to be sad, you know," she said. "Are you sad?"

I rolled back over. She was standing in my doorway, Dad holding her hand and right by her side.

The truth is, I feel beyond sad. I feel empty. Numb. When I drank, this was always how I wanted to feel.

THIRTEEN

I SHOULD HAVE SAVED the whole skipping school thing for a better day. Like today. After yesterday, with the weirdness of hanging out with Caro, of all people, and then that horrible conversation with Mom and Dad, I could have used a day off from the forced-knowledge factory.

But of course I didn't get one. Even worse, I had to face Giggles with Mom and Dad along. Apparently we'd all been summoned for a meeting.

The ride to school with them was quiet. Too quiet. No one said anything about why we were all going to school. No one said anything about last night. I expected as much. I know what I've done and I hate myself for it, so why should they be any different?

Still, I'd—I know what I did, but I guess I thought that maybe Mom and Dad would . . . not understand, not that. But I thought there might be more than the endless quiet.

When we got to school, we sat in the guidance office and waited. It's not like I haven't done it before, except then it was Julia and me, and this time it was just me. And Mom and Dad.

I might as well have been alone, though, because while we waited Dad used one of the six million gadgets his company's given him to check his e-mail. Mom wandered around for a while, then came back and flipped through college brochures, muttering things like "Emphasis on the arts? Since when?" Neither of them said anything to me.

I thought about the last time Julia and I were here. It was late last May, and Giggles had grabbed us as soon as we'd come in, loudly pointing out that we were three minutes late and then dragged us to her office for her usual "you've got detention and don't think I won't be watching you" lecture.

Julia was wearing the dress she'd made out of an old-fashioned slip we'd picked up at the Methodist church thrift store, Lawrenceville's answer to vintage. Her fingers were still stained purple from the dye she'd used to color it. In the car, she had braided her hair while we sat waiting at a traffic light, giving the drivers behind us the finger when they honked because the light had turned green, and then looped the braids into a bun knotted with purple ribbons.

She looked so amazing. All day long, people turned to watch Julia walk down the hall, and after third period Kevin apologized for his latest screwup. She laughed at him and then patted his head like he was a little kid or a dog, but forgave him at the end of the day, folding her arms across her chest the way she did when she wanted to look sure but was actually nervous.

"He loves me, I know he does, and it'll be different now, won't it?" she said afterward, and I knew the question wasn't one she wanted answered. So I tugged a hair ribbon instead, pulling it free, and her braids slipped out.

She laughed, loud and strong like she always did, and then said, "I'm supposed to go meet him, but I'm feeling the need for a trip to Millertown and some ice cream. Besides, he deserves to wait around wondering where I am. What do you say?"

We drove to Millertown. In the grocery store parking lot we sat on her car hood, eating stolen ice cream and making up stories about everyone walking by.

"When we get old, we'll go grocery shopping together every week," Julia said after a little old lady (I'd said she was a former snake handler/brothel owner) walked by. "We'll bitch about our fake hips and the weather and steal ice cream every time. Promise?"

"Promise," I said, and she smiled.

I miss her so much.

Giggles appeared after first period had started. As she swept into the room she claimed to have been "occupied elsewhere" and then said, "You know, we feel it's important to maintain contact with our students because it fosters the best atmosphere for education." Ha! I suppose lurking in the halls trying to find someone to chew out is about creating atmosphere.

Her office was the same as always, plastered with her degree from Crap U and all her certificates. (Apparently they give them for something called "Word Processing II." Pathetic.)

She then "apologized" for "having to bring yesterday's troubling matter to light," and said, "I think we should take another look at Amy's situation. As you know, her record here is spotty at best, and it may be that an alternative school, like Pinewood's vo-tech program, might be—"

"How are her grades?" Dad asked.

"Well, her grades aren't really the issue. What happened yesterday is why we're here, and I'd like—"

"You mentioned needing to take another look at Amy's situation," Dad said, his voice icy, and now I knew why whenever someone from his work called, they always sounded nervous. "Since you brought it up and mentioned an alternative school, this must mean Amy's grades are an issue. Grace and I haven't heard anything of the sort from any of her teachers, or, for that matter, you, so if you know of any academic problems, I certainly hope you'll share them with us now."

Giggles looked like someone had shoved a whole sack of lemons in her mouth. "I'm not aware of any academic problems at the moment."

"I see. So then we just need to deal with Amy's absence yesterday. A single, isolated incident. Correct?"

"Skipping school is a very serious issue."

"I completely agree with you," Mom said, putting one hand on Dad's arm. "In fact, while we were waiting to see you, I chatted briefly with a very nice woman. A Mrs. Howard? Halder? I'm afraid I'm terrible with names. I always have my students sit in alphabetical order because of it. Amy, do you know who I'm talking about? She said she works with the principal."

"Mrs. Harris?" There are many things you could call Mrs. Harris, but nice isn't one of them. Her favorite word is "No," and even though Mr. Waters is technically the school principal, everyone knows Mrs. Harris runs everything and Mr. Waters spends his time counting down the days until he can retire.

"Right," Mom said. "Anyway, Mrs. Griggles, Mrs. Harris told me that twenty-five students skipped school yesterday. She also told me that we were the only parents called in for a meeting because of it."

"Well, you see—"

"And the really funny thing," Mom continued, "is that she also told me that Amy missed twelve days of school last year. Do you know how many phone calls Colin and I received about that from you?"

Giggles looked positively full of lemons now. "Well, last year we weren't as fully staffed as we'd hoped and—"

"Of course. But I think that, in the future, it might be better if you focused less on Amy's past and more on her current situation. And now—well, surely you need to contact those twenty-four other families, and we don't want to take up any more of your time. Thank you so very much for seeing us." And then she and Dad stood up.

Giggles didn't stand up. She just sat there, totally silent for the first time ever. I would have laughed, but I couldn't actually speak myself.

My parents had told Giggles off. I'd never seen anything like it. Even Julia had only been able to get away with calling her Mrs. Giggles and then saying, "Oops, sorry, Mrs. Griggles."

They'd stood up for me. After what I'd told them, after they knew what I'd done to Julia, they'd stood up for me. I couldn't believe it.

They acted like nothing had happened, though. Even when we were out of the guidance office Mom just patted my arm quickly and said, "See you this afternoon." Dad did the same thing, only he said, "See you this evening." Then they left.

That was it. It felt like there should have been something else. I wanted there to be something else. I wanted to run after them and hug them. I wanted to say thank you.

I wanted to run after them and say that after I missed ten days of school last year I brought a letter home for them. They had to sign it, say they knew how often I'd been gone. I gave it to them after dinner, after they'd talked about their days to each other and I'd picked the meat out of my lasagna.

They were doing the dishes, which really meant they made out while they loaded the dishwasher. (There are some things no one needs to see. Parents making out is *so* one of them).

After I cleared my throat a lot, Mom pulled herself away from Dad long enough to sign it. She didn't read the letter. She just signed it and handed it to Dad, who gave it back to me. He didn't read it either.

I didn't run after them. I didn't say anything to them. I just watched them go. It was quiet in the hallway, and I thought I could hear the door click closed as they left.

I didn't really want to go to class after all that, but it wasn't like I had a choice, especially since Giggles came out into the hall and glared at me until I walked away. I walked through the cafeteria and then cut through the student resource center to reach the hall that led to my first class. Whoever "designed" Lawrenceville High wasn't much of an architect. Putting the cafeteria, resource center, and auditorium in the middle, and then branching hallways off it—it's like going to school inside a wagon wheel.

The student resource center was deserted just like always, stacks of pamphlets piled up waiting to be read (it'll never happen), and Mrs. Mullins off on one of her six zillion smoking breaks. As I pushed open the door that led into the hallway, I saw someone leaning against the far wall, almost hidden by one of the six million trophy cases scattered around the school.

It was Patrick. He was leaning against the wall, only not so much leaning as looking like he wanted to press through and get outside, get away. For some reason, I thought about asking him if he was okay, and even took an almost-step toward him, but before I could he looked at me and the expression in his eyes sent me walking away as fast as I could.

He looked relatively calm, his mouth compressed into a thin line, but his eyes—I can still see the expression in them now. He looked like I feel. He looked sad, like he'd lost something he could never get back.

He looked . . . he looked angry too.

In class, I got a tardy slip despite explaining that I'd been stuck in Giggles's office. I also got my last test back. I got an A. Written right below it was, "Only one in the class! Great work!" The last time a teacher wrote anything about me that ended with a ! and was positive, I was in middle school.

After all that, I figured my day couldn't get any worse. Or stranger.

I was totally wrong.

Mel and Beth are together. Like, actually doing the whole boyfriend-and-girlfriend thing together. I found out in English, when they walked into class holding hands. Corn Syrup came in right after they did. She looked fine. We broke into our groups and she argued with Mel and totally ignored me. She would have ignored Patrick too, if he'd been there, but he wasn't.

It was like yesterday and the stuff she said never happened. Was it all an act? Or—wait—maybe some sort of plan to—oh, forget it. I have no friends, no life, nothing. Beth wouldn't waste her time trying to get me. I'm not worth noticing. And Corn Syrup certainly wouldn't do anything on her own. Yesterday was . . .

Yesterday, she was probably just high from the fumes of her hair products or something.

Caro really did seem fine about the Mel and Beth thing. Mel was acting kind of weird though. He ignored me except to ask if I knew where Patrick was (like I'm his keeper) and spent all of class arguing with Caro and giving her these looks, like he was trying to ask her a question without saying anything.

Beth walked by just as Caro looked like she was going to say something to him, and ran her fingers along the back of his neck. Mel immediately got that stupid glazed-over expression guys get when they're thinking about getting laid.

I glanced at Caro, and she was just smiling away, grinning at Mel and Beth like they were adorable and not nauseating. I suppose if they'd started going at it she would have offered up her desk for them to use.

Beth said—to Corn Syrup, obviously, and not me, "So, what about Friday? Did you ask about Joe?"

"Not yet, but it's been, like, all I've been thinking about since you told me," Caro said, and if her smile had gotten any wider her face would have cracked. She turned to Mel. "Can you find out if Joe's going to be at Tammy's party?"

"Joe Regent?" Mel sounded shocked. Joe was this honors guy who somehow managed to make the football team. He was a big deal for them, but to me he'd always be the guy who told Julia her eyes were "like velvet" and then got all teary-eyed after she laughed at him.

Caro nodded. "He's hot, and I want to know if he's coming because . . . you know."

Mel frowned, and when the bell rang, he bolted into the hallway. Beth looked so pissed that I laughed out loud. She didn't even glance at me, of course, but Caro did. Her eyes were narrowed and unhappy-looking.

"He probably went to look for Patrick," she told Beth. Her eyes were wide and happy again.

"Yeah, I know that, Caro. I don't know why Mel still hangs out with him. What are you wearing to the party?"

"I don't know. I totally need your help." She smiled, jammed her book in her bag, tossed her hair back, and walked out with Beth. Still the perfect follower except her left hand, hanging by her side, was curled up tight, an angry silent fist. I walked behind her and Beth all the way down the hall, and Caro's hand never unknotted.

That's when I knew why yesterday happened.

Yesterday, when Caro followed me, when we hung out, Mel and Beth were already together. They must have hooked up after the movie, and I'll bet anything that yesterday morning was when Caro found out. It would be just like Beth to wait and tell her at school. To say, "Oh, I thought I told you! I mean, everyone totally knows already," and then give her every single detail so she could watch Caro's face. So everyone could see Caro's face.

Caro came after me to get away. That's why she was so upset. It wasn't because of what I said and later, us hanging out—it wasn't about me. It was about her wanting to pretend she wasn't going to go along and act like everything was fine. I was safe to talk to, safe to vent at. It was middle school all over again, except this time she didn't even have to worry that Beth might find out. The thing is—

The thing is, I thought Caro maybe wanted to be friends. Not hang-out-in-school friends or anything like that, but just . . . I don't know. That maybe we might talk sometime or something. I thought—I thought we did talk yesterday. I thought we talked for real.

I am so stupid.

124 days

J,

I swear, today has actually been three days. Every day has been like that lately.

Things with my parents are horrid. We've talked about me skipping school (How's it going now? Do you think you know why you skipped?) so much I almost want to tell them about Corn Syrup to get them to shut up. But I don't want their pity, J. I want them to just stop trying. They keep looking at me, smiling these brittle, scared smiles, and I can't stand it. I want them to stop acting like . . . I want them to stop acting like they want to be around me. I want to tell them I haven't forgotten what I told them about what I did to you and I know they haven't either. I want to ask them why they won't mention it. I want to scream at them to call me what I know I am and get it over with.

I just called your house. A fake female voice answered, the phone company politely telling me, sorry, the number I was trying to reach had been changed. The new number wasn't given.

Before, when I called, at least I knew the phone would be answered, you know? I'd hear your mother's voice. I could pretend. Now I don't even have that.

I want to go downstairs and stand in front of my parents as they sit nestled together on the sofa. Why can't they be like normal parents and drift through a room without noticing the other person is there? Why do they always have to be so together? Why is it when they look at me I want to scream until my voice is gone?

I want to force their mouths open, make them say the word *murderer*.

Why won't they say it? Why can't they just get it out there? I keep thinking about that. The why. Why they won't say what we all know is true. Why I did what I did. Why I thought getting you to see Kevin cheating on you was a good idea. Why, when you got so upset, I thought getting in your car and leaving was a good idea. Why I took your hand and smiled at you, said that everything would be okay. Why did I do it? Why?

I don't know, J. I don't. All I know is this:

You never should have been my friend.

FOURTEEN

TODAY STARTED OFF OKAY—for it being a school day, for it being 125 days without Julia—but in English, things started sucking because Beth smushed herself into our group. She must have given the teacher, Ms. Gladwell, some crap story—I wasn't listening—but when I looked up from my copy of *Huckleberry Finn* (way less boring than *The Scarlet Letter*) she was there, grinning at Mel and saying, "Caro, can you squeeze a desk in for me?"

It had better not be a permanent thing, because what followed was pure torture. Beth giggled. She swished her hair around. She whispered to Mel. She whispered to Caro. She did the "we have mysterious hand gestures that make us giggle" thing.

She has a brain in that rotten head of hers—whenever Mrs. Gladwell came around to check on our discussion, Beth would say something about the book that was pretty smart. That's the nicest thing I can say about her. She's evil, but she isn't stupid.

Beth should have some redeeming characteristics. At least one, anyway, because she is theoretically human. But there isn't a single good thing about her. If anything, she's even more of a troll than I remembered. For instance, every time Mel said something to Caro, she'd give Caro a look, an "I can ruin you in thirty seconds if I want or if I'm bored" smile.

So of course Caro never did more than mumble, "I don't know" or "I haven't really thought about that part of the book yet."

After a while, Mel gave up and tried to talk to me and Patrick. I said I hadn't done the reading even though I had (no way did I want to get sucked into a conversation with Beth). Of course it didn't work because Beth said, "Amy, you didn't do *any* of the reading?" really loudly so Gladwell would hear and which got me a "Stay after class, please." Patrick just laughed when Mel asked him, which I wished had been my answer.

Hearing Patrick laugh was strange. Aside from that night in the basement, I've never seen him look anything but tense or angry. It's like he's always on edge.

And the laugh itself? It sounded like . . . well, it sounded like he'd forgotten how to laugh.

Naturally, Beth made a face at him, and then she and Caro whispered to each other, which meant Beth looked at Patrick and me and said "Freak" loud enough for us all to hear. Corn Syrup blushed but nodded along like some sort of stupid puppet.

I wished the ground would open up and swallow them both, and looked over at Mel.

He was giving Patrick a look. A look kind of like one of Julia's, actually. The "Amy, don't start in on Guy X because I'm getting some and I like it and you're always PMSing about love anyway" one. (Except, obviously, guys don't PMS about love. And, for that matter, neither do I. Julia was the one who did, who'd get mad whenever I tried to explain that love isn't something anyone should want.)

Anyway, even though I thought Mel was a jackass for being with Beth, I couldn't help but smile. That look just reminded me so much of Julia. Plus, it was nice to know he wasn't completely oblivious of Beth's inherent trollness.

After class, Gladwell "talked" to me about "staying the course" and "working to my potential." It's like every teacher I have has some sort of " " manual to use when talking to me. She finished with, "You have so much going for you," which was the dumbest thing anyone, even Laurie, has ever said to me. I knew it was a sign the day was only going to get worse.

Naturally, it did. First, Gladwell's lecture hadn't taken long enough, and I still had to deal with part of my lunch period. I went to the cafeteria, grabbed a veggie wrap, and waited in line to pay even though my usual seat at the reject table had already been taken by mustache girl. Her seat had been taken by suit boy, who'd lost his seat to an overflow of ninth-grade girls who'd gotten invited to the jock table and were being leered at by the seniors. Fresh meat for the slaughter. I almost felt sorry for them.

Why do people think being with someone is the answer to everything? Julia hated it when I said stuff like that, but I can't help it. Thinking about one person will just turn you into my parents, and all you have to do is look at them to see that love doesn't give you a perfect life. In their case, it gave them me.

I paid for my "food," and even though I'd wished mustache girl would suddenly realize she had that thing on her lip and then rush off to bleach it, she hadn't, and so I had to wander around trying to find a seat. I passed Beth's table as I was making my way over to what looked like a vacant chair at the end of the choir table.

Yes, that's what I'm reduced to these days. Hoping the freaking choir people won't tell me, "Sorry, you can't sit here." I know it's what I deserve, but it's . . . it's hard.

Beth was talking away about her favorite subject—herself—and so of course everyone was making appropriately excited hand gestures of joy. Except Corn Syrup. She really . . . wasn't. I mean she was trying, but she clearly wasn't into it. She looked tired. Sad.

I smiled at her. It was stupid and I don't know why I did it. I guess maybe I was thinking about the stuff she said when we hung out, and how awful English class had been today. How Beth acted when Mel tried talking to her in class, threat wrapped in a smile. How defeated Caro had sounded when she'd talked about her.

How she'd said the last real conversation she'd had was years ago. With me.

Caro started to smile back, but then—well, she realized what she was about to do, and a look of terror flashed across her face. It was like I was a little kid again, standing there as she turned away, turned to Beth. I can't believe I forgot, even for a second, that she's still the same moron she always was.

I made myself move then, made myself walk off. I told myself it wasn't like I'd expected anything different, but I guess part of me had because I felt . . . I felt like I used to years ago, before Julia came along. She never would have done anything like that to me. She—and drinking—made me shinier, stronger. Julia was always there for me.

And then I knew, suddenly, what I had to do.

I dumped my tray and left the cafeteria. I heard people saying stuff—*there she goes*, whisper whisper—but for once I didn't care. I knew how to get rid of the poison Laurie had put inside me with her questions about Julia. I knew how to remember what was real. I knew how to see the way me and J truly were again. I'd finally thought of something to bring a little piece of her back.

I went to what used to be her locker and I made it Julia's again.

It felt so good when I started that I wished I'd done it sooner. I'd thought I couldn't before. I was afraid. But it was nothing to reach up and pull down all those stupid stars and messages. It was easy.

"Do you want some help?"

It was Patrick. I'd been looking around as often as possible, checking to make sure no one was in the hall, so I should have seen him coming. I mean, he's a big guy, built like the jerk jocks that shove through the school making sure everyone knows they're around. He's not like that, though. He moves like he doesn't want to be seen. It reminded me of that night, the one where I didn't see him until I tripped over him and then moved closer and closer, holding on tighter and longer than I ever have with anyone.

He wasn't standing super close or anything, but I wanted him farther away. I wanted to block him out. Block memories. His skin. His breath skittering over my ear, my throat. His question to me that night at the movies, about who I used to be and did I miss her, that girl that once was.

"I'm fine," I said, and my voice—it shook. It cracked. Outside I am tall, but inside I am so small. So weak.

"She wasn't really a foil star poetry kind of person, was she?" he said, and pointed at the flood of fake stars and words scattered around my feet.

"Nope," I said, grinding one shoe into a heart sparkling with Beth's name. (No message, of course. Just her name—BETH—in glittery letters.) And then, when I realized what he said, "You knew her?"

He pulled a star off her locker. "Not really. But she . . . she stood out. And we talked once."

"She never told me."

He handed me the star. I waited for him to say something else, but he didn't, just unpeeled and unstuck and caught the door after I yanked it open. It smelled like Julia for just a second, a hint of her under the scent of glue and ink spelling out messages she'd never see, and I felt dizzy with how much I missed her.

I stuck one hand inside to steady myself and found something. On the top shelf, wedged back in the corner, I found a pot of lip gloss, one Julia bought when we went to the beauty supply store with her mom's credit card the day after Thanksgiving last year, the one she loved in the store but hated when we got outside because instead of deep red it was a dark brownish orange, a shade no one could ever wear.

I remember when she put it in her locker. "To remind me," she said, "that everyone makes mistakes. Even me." Then she grinned, so wide, and pulled out two little liquor bottles.

She waved them at me, teasing, and then we snuck into the bathroom. She laughed when I reached for the second while I was still drinking the first, and I laughed too because I knew she'd give it to me, knew Julia would—

"Amy?"

I was holding Julia's lip gloss so hard that I'd cracked the case, and color had smeared across my palm like sickness on my skin. I stared at it, but it didn't go away. I wanted Julia to come along and smile, make me take my sleeve and rub my skin clean. I wanted Julia to make a face at the lip gloss and toss it over her shoulder, not caring if it landed in a trash can or on the floor. I wanted her there.

I wanted to know why Julia never said anything about my drinking. I'd lied to Laurie. Whenever I threw up or fell down Julia never said a word. She would help me back up. She would get me water. She would pass me tissues or paper towels or an old sweater from the back of her car. She would do all that, but she never said a word.

She would always hand me a bottle when I asked.

Patrick touched my hand and I looked at him. He looked startled, was staring at his fingers sliding across the color marking me like he didn't know his own skin.

"It's broken," he said, and even though I saw him speak, his voice was so quiet I could hardly hear him. His hand was freezing, his fingers like icicles against my skin. I pulled away from him.

"It's hers," I said. I said it again, louder, but there was no one around to listen. He was already gone and I just stood there, Julia's lip gloss melting into my skin.

Giggles found me, still standing there, after the bell rang. She marched me to her office. She made me wash my hands. She wouldn't give the lip gloss back. When she was done talking at me and said I had to go see Mr. Waters, I saw her sweep it off her desk and into her trash can.

I felt something twist sharp inside me when she did that. Why did that one small piece of Julia have to go? My vision spotted yellow and black, and I wanted to scream, "Give it back. GIVE IT BACK!"

I didn't. I wish I had. I fixed Julia's locker, but that's nothing. Nothing.

Mr. Waters said my parents had been called and then told me he wanted a 2,500-word essay about respecting others.

"Because of your, uh, situation," he said, glancing at Mrs. Harris to make sure he was saying the right thing, "I think this would be most helpful to you. And we do want to help you, you know."

He didn't ask why I did it. No one did. No one asked, and no one saw that I just wanted to bring part of Julia back.

FIFTEEN

130 DAYS.

It feels like nothing and forever at the same time. I'd ask Laurie about it, but there's no point.

I wish I didn't have to see her every week. I wish I didn't have to see her at all. I guess Mom or Dad (probably both) must have called and told her about me skipping school and the locker thing because the first words out of her mouth as soon as I sat down were, "Why don't you tell me what's been going on at school?"

Yeah, like I needed to hear the pen clicking about that. I ignored her and fished around in my backpack instead. I wished I'd taken one of the waiting room magazines, because then I could have read it in front of her. All I had with me was homework—which I wasn't desperate enough to do—and the notebook I write to Julia in. I pulled it out and clicked my pen a few times.

"We can talk about something else, if you'd like," she said, and I smiled to myself. I knew the pen clicking would work.

"How about your notebook?" she said. "I've noticed you always have it with you. What's it for?"

"Nothing." I tried to make my voice as bored as possible, so she wouldn't keep asking about it.

She looked at me. I looked back. She clicked her pen (argh!) and said, "All right, let's move on. I've asked you to think about Julia and your friendship with her, and we've discussed certain events."

Meaning the . . . she meant that thing we'd talked about before, and I wasn't doing that. No way. I jammed the notebook back into my bag and wished it was her big stupid head.

"You look upset," she said.

"I'm fine," I said, and looked at the clock. Still forever to go.

I wished Laurie would just shut up and put me on drugs. I'd take anything to avoid dealing with her every week. They tried that when I first got to Pinewood, actually. Put me on antidepressants. The first one really messed with me—I spent two days in the bathroom in what was called "severe gastrointestinal distress." (Only doctors would have a fancy name for that.)

Then I got put on another pill, only that one made me so nauseated that I couldn't eat. Or rather, I could, but then I'd just throw it right back up. I refused to take anything after that, but the med people called my parents (called a "consultation," of course, so it could cost more) and suggested some stuff I'd never heard of.

Well, when they did that, my mother, who never met a subject she couldn't research to death, said she wanted to think about it, and called back later that day to say, sorry, she didn't want her daughter on antipsychotics, thank you. I definitely wasn't crazy about taking something like that either (ha!), but the next day I had my first session with Laurie, and by the end of it I was willing to take anything to get away from her and her questions. I told her that the med people had suggested some drugs and I'd go ahead and take them and skip out on therapy.

"Hmmmm," she'd said, clicking her damn pen, and that was the end of that. No drugs for me, just lots of talking. If I'd known things would have ended up like this, I would have stayed on the vomit pills.

"Did any of the things that have happened to you at school have to do with Julia?"

She knew they did. *She knew.* I could practically hear her itching to ask more questions and click her stupid pen.

"No," I said, and we sat in silence after that. I wanted to get my notebook out and write to Julia but I knew she'd be all over that and I didn't want her ruining it with her questions.

When forty-seven of our fifty minutes were up, she said, "About the notebook you carry. Is it a journal?"

I ignored her, because I knew better than to say, "No, it's letters to Julia." The amount of pen clicking that would produce—it made my head hurt just thinking about it.

"Amy, before you go, let's talk about choices for just a second."

Too bad I knew she wasn't going to be asking me if I wanted to choose to stop seeing her.

"Have you been to Julia's grave since the funeral?" she said in a totally mild voice, like she was asking about the weather or something. I looked at her then, and I . . .

I didn't say anything. I couldn't have even if I'd wanted to. The only thing that would have come out would have been a scream.

"Maybe you should think about going sometime, or consider why you haven't," she said, and then told me she'd see me next week.

How did she know I haven't been? How?

130 days

J,

Laurie wants me to come see you, but I—even at the funeral, I couldn't look at you. Everyone else did, filed by in a snaking line, the church loud with tears and footsteps. I couldn't do it. I couldn't stand up, couldn't join the line. You were lying in a shiny wooden box, and it was so wrong that you were there that I couldn't move. I just sat there, staring. I wish I hadn't been able to breathe.

But I was, and I did, and I rode in silence in the back of my parents' car to the cemetery. I had to leave when they put—when that shiny box was lowered into the ground. I went and sat on the back of the car. I stared at the sun until my eyes hurt, till everything was a bright, painful blur.

Your mother left before the service was over. I know because I could still hear the minister's voice off in the distance. Off where you were. Your mother was crying, leaning against a woman I knew was your aunt Ellen (she looked just like you described her, right down to the mole on her neck). When she saw me, she stopped crying.

She stopped crying and looked at me. She didn't tell me I shouldn't have come. She didn't have to. She didn't tell me it was all my fault. She didn't have to do that either. She just looked at me. I wish she had done something— said something, anything. But she didn't. She just looked at me, and then she turned away.

I haven't been to see you because I can't. I just can't but . . .

But Laurie knew, J. She knows how weak I am.

SIXTEEN

I CLOSED MY NOTEBOOK and ignored Mom's glances at it. I knew she wouldn't ask what I was writing.

And she didn't. Instead, all the way home I had to answer questions about school. Ever since I fixed Julia's locker, I get questions from her and Dad all the time.

So I talked.

I said, "Yes, classes are fine."

I said, "Yes, I'm trying to make friends." (I don't know how to. I should have tried at Pinewood, maybe. But I couldn't. I didn't deserve to, and besides, without Julia, without alcohol, I was shrunken, silent, back to being that little kid who knew the right words would never come.)

All the way home it was like that, question after question, and I knew that when Mom and I went inside there would be praise over me doing my homework and putting my dishes in the sink after dinner and maybe even a hug or two. All those things I was once so sure I wanted.

Now all I want is for them to stop, for Mom and Dad to be like they were, happy and in love and me in orbit around them.

They still haven't said a word about what I told them about Julia the other night. They still won't say what I did. What I am.

"I want to . . . I need to go to the cemetery," I said to Mom as she pulled into the driveway. She looked over at me, and I knew I had to say more.

"Laurie said I should." I thought that would be enough, the magic words, but she just kept looking at me.

"You can call and ask her, if you want," I added, and thought about how I used to dream of Mom looking at me like she was now, listening to me. Wanting to hear more. Wanting to hear me.

I never wanted it like this, though.

Mom bit her lip. "Do you want to go?"

"I've never been to see her. I . . . I haven't even seen her grave. The day of the funeral I couldn't—"

"Amy," my mother said gently, so gently, like those three letters were fragile, lovable. I stared down at my hands. They were balled into fists on my lap, and I knew if I moved they would too. Once upon a time I would have given anything—and I mean anything, even nights out partying with Julia—to hear her talk to me like that.

"You don't have to do this to yourself," she said.

I knew if I moved something would happen. I could feel it inside me, in my fists still clenched in my lap. I had to push down a surge of something bitter clawing at my throat and burning behind my eyes.

"Laurie really did say I should do it."

"I believe you, and I'm sure she has her reasons. But Laurie wasn't there the day of the funeral. She didn't see . . . she didn't see your face. She didn't see you in the car, in the church. When your father and I came back to the car after, I thought . . . I thought, 'That's what a ghost looks like.' You were so—" She broke off suddenly, breath shuddering.

I looked over at her. She was staring straight ahead, blinking hard and fast. The edges of her eyes were red.

"Please take me," I said, loving and hating how upset she was, loving and hating that I'd caused it.

She did.

When we got there, she agreed to let me go in alone but wouldn't let me walk back home by myself. "I know it's not that far, but I'm waiting for you. I won't leave you."

I didn't want those words from her, not like that, not there, but at the same time I wanted them so badly that if I could have plucked them from the air, swallowed them down, and let them swim inside me, I would have.

I got out of the car and walked toward Julia.

I was the only person around, my footsteps the only sound. And then I was there, I saw where Julia was. Is. It was so . . . it was so bare. It was just ground and a stone, and there were others just like it right next to it, all around it. All around me, everywhere I looked, there was grass and stones and I—

I couldn't look at it. I couldn't bear to see the piece of ground that was hers, the stone with her name on it. I turned away and walked through the cemetery, pretended I couldn't see all those stones or the too neatly trimmed grass. I came out at the other end of the parking lot, Mom's car out of sight.

I wanted to cry but the tears wouldn't come. I could feel them, a hot burn stinging my eyes again, but something else, memories of that last night, Julia's last night, were clawing at me, leaving me standing there frozen.

I don't know how long I stood there, but after a while a car pulled into the lot. It was bright yellow, driven by an older man. When he got out, he looked as out of place as his car did, stood hesitating like he was waiting for something. Hoping for something. When he realized I was looking at him, he walked into the cemetery.

Another car pulled into the lot, but I didn't look. I just kept watching the man. His shoulders slumped and his head bowed as soon as he started walking among the graves. He looked like he belonged then.

"Amy?"

I turned around.

Julia's mother was there, staring at me like I was a bad dream. It was a weekday, almost evening, and she was supposed to be at work, her hair shellacked into place and her Assistant Store Manager tag clipped onto her smock. I knew her schedule like I knew Julia's. CostRite Pharmacy owned her now. She wasn't supposed to be standing just a few feet away from me.

But she was, leaning against her car like it was the only thing holding her up. There was a bunch of plastic-wrapped yellow flowers in her other hand. They had to be for Julia, but they were so wrong.

"Julia hates yellow," I said.

It's true—she was convinced it made her look terrible (it didn't)—but it wasn't the right thing to say. It wasn't even what I wanted to say. I hadn't talked to Julia's mother since the night I'd taken Julia's hand and said everything would be okay. Why didn't I say what I'd been trying to for so long, what I'd tried to say every time I called Julia's house?

"She probably hates being dead more," Julia's mother said, pushing away from the car.

"I didn't mean—"

"I know exactly what you meant. You knew her better than I did. Are you happy now, Amy? She wouldn't trust me with anything, even something as stupid as what color she likes, but she trusted you. She trusted you and you—"

"I know I never should have let her drive. We should have . . . I should have . . . I swear I never would have done any of it if I'd known what—"

"But you did do it. You let her drive, and now she's gone. She'll never turn eighteen, she'll never finish high school. She'll never . . . I'd give everything I've ever had or will to hear her voice again, even if it's to tell me to go to hell. But I'll never have that, will I?"

"I've tried to call, I've wanted to say—"

"I don't want to hear it," she said, and walked toward me. When she was so close I could see her foundation cracking in the lines around her eyes, see how it didn't hide the dark circles under them, she stopped and grabbed my arm. "I don't want to hear from you, I don't want to see you. I've lost everything because of you. Everything."

"I'm sorry," I said, and finally, finally it came out. Finally I said it. "I'm so sorry for what I did."

"You're sorry?" She dropped my arm like my skin burned her. "You're sorry? She was my world. Your words, your 'sorry,' what does it do? She's still gone, and you're still here." She hit me with the flowers, the plastic smacking my face, petals flying into the air around us. "Keep your words. They aren't enough. They won't ever be enough."

I ran then, turned and stumbled my way across the parking lot, toward Mom's car and Mom sitting calmly inside, smiling like she was glad to see me. I said I had a headache and lay down in the backseat, pressed my face into it and wished it would swallow me whole.

130 days

I saw you, J. I saw your mother too, and she . . . well, what she said to me is true. Sorry is just a word, and a word can't make things right. It can't change what I did. It can't bring you back.

Mom knew something happened, I guess, because when we got home, she came up to my room and checked on me every five minutes till I finally gave up and went downstairs. I floated, numb, through homework and dinner, saying yes, I was fine, when both Mom and Dad asked, and then cried the tears I couldn't before in bed. I didn't feel better afterward.

I knew I wouldn't.

I can't sleep. I've been lying here for hours and hours thinking about the cemetery. About your mother's face. About what she said. About your grave.

I'm thinking about you. Remember when we went to Splash World? You totally scammed us inside and even got us onto all the best rides without waiting. We bought cotton candy and ate horrible seven-dollar hot dogs. We got our picture taken with Swimmy the Seal.

I still have the picture. I'm smiling in it. You're standing in front of me. Your face is a blur because you'd turned toward me, the camera capturing you like you were, always in motion. The side of your mouth is open, laughing, and you're leaning in a bit, like you're going to rest your head on my shoulder.

You did. You always did that when I made you laugh or when someone else made you sad.

I've thought about that day, and about the time we tried to make caramel in your kitchen and had to open all the windows to get rid of the horrible burnt-sugar smell. I've thought about all the times I rode to school in your car, digging around on the floor through the pile of CDs you'd burned and how no matter which one I picked there was always at least one stupid love song that you knew all the words to. I've thought about all the times I lay on your bed, watching you make faces as you talked on the phone.

I've thought about how you would make me knock on the door and pretend to be your mother if it was a guy you didn't want to talk to, and the way we'd laugh afterward. I've thought about all the times we walked down the hallways at school and you'd whisper, "Amy, you're model tall. Model! Show it off! I didn't loan you my T-shirt so you could do the slouchy hiding thing, you know."

I've thought about what Laurie asked me.

That night, the one with the guy with mean eyes and the grain alcohol? You knew. I know that now. I can—I can say it. You knew. You knew everything. You said you were scared afterward. I know what that means. I think maybe I always did. You meant you were sorry.

I think Laurie would say that means something. I think she would say it means something big. I think she would say it means you hurt me.

I think it means you were sorry.

People aren't just one thing, you know? They aren't all good or all bad, and what Laurie wants me to see is true—you did hurt me—but it's only part of the truth.

The truth is that you were strong and fierce and funny. The truth is that you had terrible taste in guys. (And in music too, you and all your love songs.) The truth is that you would loan me anything of yours I wanted—even if you'd just gotten it—and never ask for it back. I still have your "My Broom Is in the Shop" tee in my closet.

I was always afraid to wear it, but I wanted to. And you knew it. Without me ever saying so, you knew it and gave it to me.

The truth is that night, the night I picked up my bottle and swallowed grain alcohol, you knew what I was drinking when I didn't.

The truth is that when I got sick, when I closed my eyes and faded away, you were there. You took me to the hospital. You didn't leave me. You were there for me.

Yeah, it's true that you never told me to stop drinking. And yeah, it's true that you helped me drink.

But I chose to. Every time—every single time—it was always my choice. Mine. Not yours.

The truth is I'm the one who drank. I'm going to tell Laurie that next time I see her.

Maybe she'll even listen.

SEVENTEEN

IT FIGURED that the one time I actually wanted to see Laurie she wasn't around.

"But you just saw her two days ago," Dad said when he picked me up after school and I asked if I could see her again.

From the way he was looking at me, I knew he and Mom had already talked to Laurie about my visit to Julia's grave.

I gritted my teeth and said, "I know, but I need to see her again."

I was willing to put up with anything to see the look on Laurie's face when I blew her stupid questions about Julia back in her face.

"All right," Dad said, but after we got home (and he'd talked to Mom, of course) he called Laurie's office and found out that Laurie's father is sick and she's gone out of town. So there's no way I can see her now, plus my appointment for next week has been canceled. It's weird to think of Laurie having parents. I would have thought she just hatched fully grown with a clicking pen in one hand.

Mom, who was home for the afternoon because she'd given her classes the day off to work on their papers, started to suggest I go see Dr. Marks, the group therapy leader at Pinewood. Apparently he has a private practice. (I can just see it now. Me, him, and the ever-changing parade of food in his mustache.)

I cut her off before she could finish and asked her if she wanted to go to the mall. I knew that would stop her trying to get me to see Mustache Man, and it did.

"This is wonderful," Mom said, sounding so pleased, and I stared at her until she looked away. Looked at Dad.

Julia's mother drove her crazy, but she wanted J in her life. She loved her so much. I've been thinking about her a lot since I saw her. I know it's not possible, but I wish I could talk to her. Really talk to her, I mean. Talk to her about Julia. She knows what it's like to miss her. She knows how wrong a world without Julia in it is and isn't afraid to say it.

She isn't afraid to say what's true.

My parents, however, are.

They still haven't said anything about what happened—about what I did—and while Mom was getting her purse I wondered if they ever will.

I could ask. I know that. But I don't.

Mom came back and said, "Ready to go?"

"Ready," I said, and I don't ask because I don't want to hear their answer. I want to pretend I could be a daughter they could want even though I know I'm not. Never have been, never will be.

As soon as we got to the mall, Mom pressed one of her charge cards into my hands and told me to go shopping.

"I know you probably don't want to run into people from school with your mom around," she said, a huge smile on her face. "So go have fun, buy yourself some clothes. You must be tired of wearing those outfits we got after you—before you went back to school."

She smiled again, too wide. "Meet me in the food court in an hour and if you want to stay longer and talk to your friends, that's fine with me. I told your father we might be late."

"I'll be back in thirty," I said, and took off. I wanted a break from her, from how happy she was that I'd let her take me somewhere, but there was no way I could spend an hour in the mall. It reminded me too much of Julia, of the way things used to be.

I avoided all the stores we went in, which left me with the stationery store, with its cutesy fake-homemade cards, and the kitchen store. I went in the kitchen store and walked around looking at the pots and pans and twelve dollar jars of salsa. It was very boring, even with a huge candy display at the back of the store, and after what felt like three hours, the cutting-edge and very expensive clock on display said ten minutes had passed. I moved on to looking at vinegars. That took three minutes, and that included reading the back of one of the bottles. (Apparently organic vinegar is necessary if you really want to "taste the flavor" of your food. Go figure.)

I'd saved the candy for last but it was "old-fashioned" stuff involving a lot of dried fruit. There was a ton of it, though, and after a while I found something with chocolate and marshmallows that looked edible. I could almost hear J saying, "Finally! Real food!"

I went through the whole stack of boxes twice before picking one up. It looked like all the others, but choosing that one meant that by the time I was done the clock showed twenty-three minutes had passed.

Then it hit me. What was I going to do with the candy? Buy it? Julia wasn't there to share it with, to pick off the marshmallow parts and eat them first like she did with s'mores. The store's cash register froze up as I stood there, and I watched it spit a long trail of receipts into the air.

The salesperson, who was about Julia's mom's age and had her color hair, bright bottle blond, looked like she was going to burst into tears. I had to put the candy down and leave then. I don't know why. It wasn't because I thought I was going to cry or anything. I just . . . I felt bad, seeing that woman's face. Being there, in the mall, without Julia.

I should have run into someone from school then. A big dramatic moment, straight out of one of those crappy movies J used to love to watch. A run-in with mustache girl, maybe. We could have exchanged glances, both of us knowing that shopping alone on a weekday afternoon wasn't normal. It couldn't ever pass as normal.

But I didn't see mustache girl. I didn't see anyone, and I walked back to Mom. She was talking on her cell when I got to the food court, facing away from me with one arm propped up on a table, head resting on her hand as she talked.

I used to sit like that when I talked to Julia.

"I'm trying," she said. "It's just difficult. She still hasn't said a word to me about visiting Julia's grave. Has she said anything to—? No, I know you'd tell me if she had. I just . . . I hoped. Right, I know. All she said was 'Fine' on the way here, Colin. No matter what I ask, that's always her answer. I don't know what she's thinking. I look at her and . . . "

She should have realized I was behind her. Heard me breathing. Seen the shadow I cast. But of course she didn't. "I don't know her," she said. "How can she be such a stranger to me? Why can't I—? No, honey, I'm fine. I am. I just wish you and I—"

I left the mall. I didn't want to hear her wishes. I could already guess what they were.

Outside, I went to the bus stop and stood next to two women with elaborate makeup and tired eyes. They discussed work schedules and how to sell moisturizer. They both told me I was lucky to be so tall. I sat behind them on the bus and listened to them all the way to the transfer stop, where they got off. I stayed on, resting my head against the window, and watched the sky turn dark.

Corn Syrup got on the bus my second time through the transfer stop. Her pep squad uniform was poking out of her bag just so, as if everyone on their way from work would be impressed by the fact that she's a second-rate cheerleader. She looked washed out under the bleary lights that blinked on as passengers climbed aboard, like a shadow of herself. She paid her fare and sat down on one of the seats that face sideways, the single seats that are supposed to be for old people or pregnant women. I could almost hear Julia laughing at that. We both knew bus etiquette real well.

I missed riding the bus with Julia. I hated it when we did it, couldn't wait for J to get her car, but now . . . now I would have given anything to have her sitting next to me.

An angry-looking pregnant woman got on at the commuter rail station and asked Caro, "So when is your baby due?" with a smile that was just bared teeth. Corn Syrup got up, apologizing and tripping over herself, and looked around for a seat. I watched her spot her choices. Next to a fat man sprawled out with the paper, bulk and newsprint spreading over a seat and three-quarters, or next to me.

She picked me. When she sat down, she held her bag close to her chest, biting her lip. Julia would have said, "Hi!" and stared at her until she looked away. I looked out the window. It was dark enough that I couldn't see much of anything, and we rode in silence for what felt like a thousand years. (It was probably only nine hundred.)

No one pulled the cord for her stop, so she had to lean across me to do it. She mumbled, "Excuse me," in a snotty voice, but the effect was totally ruined when the bus hit a pothole and her head smacked into the seat in front of us.

I didn't laugh. I was going to, probably, but she didn't give me a chance. Before I could do anything she'd straightened up, hands clenched around her bag again, and said, "You know our group project? For English? We should all meet at the university library this Saturday. They have to let anyone use it because it's a state school, right?"

I shrugged. She was right about being able to use the library but I didn't want to encourage conversation, especially since I could guess what was coming.

My silence didn't stop her.

"I was thinking maybe you could come."

"Why?"

"It's a group project."

"Right. So that's why, in class, you and Mel spend all your time asking me what I think."

"We're all getting graded and we all have to—"

"Sure, that's it. Come on. You want me there because of Beth."

"It's not like that."

"Please. If just you and Mel meet, Beth will make it so you'll be stuck eating lunch with people like me."

She sighed. "Fine. You're right. Look, I'm—I'm on the bus now because Mel asked me if I wanted to meet up this weekend before practice. Beth heard and told me she couldn't give me a ride home."

"And what, that surprised you? I could have told you your ass would be on the bus for talking to Beth's property without her permission, and I haven't spoken to her in years."

Caro was silent for a moment. "Amy, about the other day—"

"What about it? I was bored, I got a meal out of listening to you whine—no big deal."

"Right," she said tightly. "So what about Saturday?"

"What about it?"

"I'm begging, okay? I can't work on our presentation with just Mel."

She sounded so miserable, and for a second I felt sorry for her. But only for a second. "Patrick will be there."

"He won't show up, or if he does, he'll leave after ten minutes or something. You know he hardly ever does anything, and this certainly isn't going to be any different. And look, it's not like group work is optional. We all have to give this presentation. And I can't deal with what will happen if—" Her voice cracked.

"Fine." I so didn't want to go through another round of Caro's dumb Beth thing. It would just remind me of my stupidity the other day.

"Really?"

"Sure," I said, but I didn't mean it. If Patrick could skip out early, I could skip the whole thing. If nothing else, it would bring my A average down to something more familiar.

"Great," she said, and relaxed her stranglehold on her bag. "So should we meet up at, like, ten? On the library steps?"

"Whatever."

She was silent for a minute as the bus slowed down and then spoke in a rush as the brakes squealed us to a stop. "I'm going to get breakfast at Blue Moon before. I'll be there around nine. If you want . . . you could meet me there."

She stood up before I could ask her if she was having

an aneurysm. I stared at the bus floor, with its covering of rail ticket stubs and crumpled newspapers, until the bus started moving again. At the next stop, I got off and called home.

Dad and Mom both came to get me. Dad was driving. He kept his head turned away when I got in the car, but as I sat down I got a glimpse of his face in the rearview mirror. His eyes were red and swollen.

Mom said, "I don't think what you've done is something to smile about, Amy."

I reached up and touched my face. There was a grin stretching across it, so wide and sharp my fingers skimmed across the edges of my gritted teeth.

On the way home she asked where I'd gone and why. I told her about the bus. I didn't mention Corn Syrup.

"Why did you leave the mall?" Dad asked as we pulled into the driveway. In the dark his eyes looked fine.

"I don't know."

"You don't know? Amy, we understand that you need your space, but your mother and I—"

"I left because she was on the phone with you, talking about me. You know, the stranger you two live with. The killer."

"Amy—" Mom said, but I tossed her credit card at her and got out of the car before I could hear her say anything else. If there's one thing I know, it's how little words mean, and right then I didn't want to hear any more of them.

Right then I knew that I couldn't.

135 days

Hey J,

It's Saturday night, but when I told Mom and Dad I was going to study in my room after dinner, they didn't say, "Are you sure you don't want to call someone and go out?" or "Maybe you could take a break later and watch a movie with us."

That's right, I'm spared an evening watching Mom and Dad snuggle on the sofa. The reason for this freedom? I went to the stupid library to work with my stupid English group on our stupid project.

I wasn't planning on going, but when I got up this morning Mom had made chocolate chip muffins and Dad was looking through the *Lawrenceville Parks and Leisure* guide, and it was so—the whole scene should have been under glass in a museum. Or on television. Mom with fresh-baked muffins! Dad planning a family outing! Rehabilitated teenager standing in the kitchen ready to embrace family *and* life!

All I need is to be six inches shorter, bustier, with normal-colored hair, and the ability to act like I believe in these moments they keep trying to create.

I know what you're thinking. Yeah, Amy, how horrible to have parents who are always so nice! What a burden to have them look so hopeful when you do something as stupid as refill someone's juice glass as you're taking the carton to the table!

What a blessing that they never expected or wanted anything from me until after they had to see me with glass in my hair and listen while an ER doctor told them what it meant, that I'd been there when my best friend died. What a blessing to hear your mother screaming for you even though you'd never answer before turning to me with hate-filled eyes. What a blessing to haunt my parents' house but never have them really see me until newspaper stories ran featuring a photo taken by Kevin, bleary-eyed me leaning against a tree with a bottle pressed to my lips as you stood next to me, smiling bright-eyed and beautiful at the camera. (An hour later, the photo would have shown you with pinholes for eyes, your forehead blister hot, slurring that no, Kevin promised it was good shit before you threw up everywhere.)

Too late, too late, juice pouring does not a kind soul make, and I killed you.

I had to get out of the house after that. When they asked me where I was going, I didn't look at their faces as I told them. I didn't want to see the smiles, the relief in their eyes. I turned down the offer of a ride. I did take the twenty bucks Dad said he wanted to give me.

You already know where this is going, don't you? You know I probably would have gone to meet Caro if there hadn't been any muffins or grateful looks when I poured juice.

You know that if you had never moved to town I would be just like her.

I don't want to understand how she feels, I don't. But I do.

EIGHTEEN

WHEN I GOT TO BLUE MOON, it was too early for students to be there, but Corn Syrup was right up front, sitting by herself at a table by the window. She was pretending to read a book. I know because when she saw me walk up, her eyes got wide and flicked from me to the page and then back again. Then she waved, one of those small ones you do when you aren't sure the other person will wave back.

I didn't wave back, but I went inside. Don't get me wrong, I knew what was going on. It was okay for her to eat breakfast with me outside of school when it was too early for anyone she knows to show up and see her. It was okay for her to talk to me about class, for us to wonder how we're going to fill a ten-minute presentation. It was even okay for us to talk about her parents and sister. For some reason, I even mentioned Mom and Dad, the morning o' muffins, and gratitude for juice pouring.

"That must be weird," she said.

I pushed a piece of pancake around on my plate. "What do you mean?"

"Well, you know, having them be all over you. They used to be so into each other."

"Still are."

"Really?"

"Yep."

"Wow. I remember when we were little and I'd come over to play, they'd say, "Go outside and have fun!" and then actually let us do that and not check in every ten seconds like my mom did. Plus the day we tried to climb up to the roof—do you remember that?—I went in to get a drink of water and they were, um, making out in your living room."

She cleared her throat. "Anyway, Mom used to talk about how you'd follow her around the kitchen whenever you came over and she was making dinner. She thought it was so great that you asked if you could help and then did. She always said . . ." She trailed off.

"What?" I'd massacred my piece of pancake into nothing, and my fork slipped across the plate.

Caro bit her lip. "She said you always seemed so lonely."

"Oh." I put my fork down and pushed my plate away, resting my hands in my lap, palms down and pressing into my knees.

"I didn't mean to—look, she's crazy. She's convinced that if I stand up straighter I'll get a boyfriend. Really, that's what she says." She laughed but it was soft, weak sounding, and I could tell she knew what her mother had said wasn't crazy at all. I pushed my hands down harder, as if I could press through my jeans, my skin, my bones, and into something else, something more solid, more real.

I wanted to tell her that what happened at breakfast with my parents wasn't weird, it was awful. I wanted to tell her that I hated them for trying so hard and hated myself for how much part of me wants to believe that they love me as much as they love each other.

I wanted to smack her, hard, and tell her to wake up, go after Mel, grab life and live it like Julia did. I wanted to tell her that people like me and her aren't really living at all. We're just here. I was lucky. I got Julia, even if it wasn't for as long as I thought. Even though I ruined it.

"We should go," I said, and got up, dug around in my pockets and found the twenty, dropped it on the table.

"That's too much," Caro said, but I was already gathering my stuff and heading for the door.

She came after me. I was heading away from the university, walking toward home and those stupid muffins, when she grabbed my arm.

"You have to come or Beth will destroy me," she said, and in that moment I actually liked her. She didn't pretend she wanted to pay me back for her breakfast or act like she cared about what she'd said. She told me the truth. She needed me to come with her because when she talked to Beth, she had to bitch about me being there so she could be safe.

So I went to the university library with her. Mel was already there, perched outside on the stairs waving his arms around like he was talking to someone even though he was alone. Caro let out a little sigh when we saw him.

"I bet if you tried, he could be yours by the end of the day," I said.

"I don't want him," she said, and before I could laugh, added, "Oh. He's not talking to himself. Patrick showed up. I didn't think he would."

Patrick was indeed there, sitting beside the huge book-drop bin, almost totally hidden from view. Inside, Mel said something about being closer to the reference databases as we grabbed a table by a window and near a door, but it was obvious that wasn't the reason why because Patrick practically threw himself into the chair closest to the window and then stared out it like he wanted to be gone.

I wondered if that was how I looked to other people. How I acted. Maybe it should have bothered me, but it didn't. Patrick looked uncomfortable with life, and I knew that feeling.

Mel sat across from him and next to me. Caro sat across from me. They didn't talk at first, but within three minutes they were arguing and we'd been glared at by a couple of bleary-eyed students slumped over laptops. After a while, they went off to look something up, still arguing, leaving me with Patrick.

It was just like being alone. He didn't talk, and every time I glanced at him—Caro wanted me to look through a list of things she'd written down, and it was so boring— he was staring out the window. Mel and Caro came back after a while, still arguing and clearly having a good time doing it because both of them were fighting back smiles as they talked.

"We can look at the other articles. I'm just asking you to—" Mel said.

"No, you were telling me there's only one way to talk about the Mississippi River's role in the book."

"I'm not. I swear! It's just that Patrick worked really hard on the multimedia presentation and I don't think we should ask him to change—"

"I can put in other stuff," Patrick said without turning away from the window. "Just tell me what you want."

Both Mel and Caro shut up for about thirty seconds before wandering off again, their hands almost, but not quite, touching. I swear, I could practically see sparks flying around them. It was sweet in a nauseating way, and I couldn't help but wonder why Mel had hooked up with Beth when it was so clear he liked Caro more.

"She told him Caro hated him."

I glanced over at Patrick. He was looking at me.

"Beth did, I mean," he said.

I laughed because of course she did. Classic Beth. She'd done that with me and Gus DePrio when we were in fifth grade and she'd decided he should be her boyfriend instead of mine. How stupid are guys that they fall for the same crap they did when we were ten?

Patrick's mouth twitched at the corners, and then he was smiling. Really smiling, and suddenly I felt like I had to look away. But I couldn't.

"Amy," he said, and Patrick's voice is—it's different. It's deep, this low rumble, but it's not loud. He speaks so quietly, like everything is a secret. Like you're the only person he wants listening. "About the other day and Julia's locker—I know I disappeared when the bell rang." He glanced away, looking back out the window. "I shouldn't have done that. I just . . . my parents—my mother—she's got so much to deal with already. But that's not—I still should have stayed, and I'm sorry I didn't."

I shrugged and stared at the table. Him saying my name made me feel weird. Him saying Julia's name made me feel weird. Him talking to me made me feel weird.

"Did it make you feel better, getting rid of everything people wanted to tell her?"

"What?" I looked at him. He wasn't looking out the window anymore. He was looking at me.

"I didn't—it wasn't like that. Nothing anyone said was real. It was just stuff they thought they should say or that their friends said."

As soon as I said it, I realized how stupid it sounded. How false. Lots of people knew Julia, liked her, and their missing her was real. I hadn't thought about that. Maybe I hadn't wanted to. I felt my face heat up.

"I did it for her."

He didn't say anything for a moment. "Can you at least walk by her locker now?"

"Shut up," I said, standing up and grabbing my stuff, and my voice sounded strange, crackly and raw. I walked out of the library, across campus, home. When I got there, I smiled and told my parents I'd had a great time.

I haven't walked by Julia's locker since I fixed it. I thought I'd be able to, but I can't. I don't . . . I don't think what I did to it was for her. I think it was for me. But fixing her locker didn't make me feel better. It didn't make Julia being gone easier to bear.

144 days

J—

Laurie's back. I saw her this afternoon. I wasn't going to say anything about her dad, but she looked really tired and sad and I felt . . . well, I actually felt sorry for her.

"I hope your father's okay," I said as I sat down, and she said, "He's much better, thank you." When I looked at her she looked back at me steadily, and I saw that although her father might be better now, he wouldn't be for long, and before I knew it, I'd told her everything about the day I visited the cemetery. Even the stuff about your mom.

"It sounds like it was very intense."

I nodded.

"What about the things she said to you?"

I shrugged.

"Do you think Julia would say them?"

"No. She wasn't like that. She would never—forget it." Typical Laurie not getting it, not seeing who you were. "There's some other stuff I have to tell you too."

I told her what I'd realized that night, about how drinking was my choice. It felt so great to finally tell her, to point out something she hadn't seen, but do you know what she said?

"Good."

That was it? Good? "But you said—you asked me all that stuff about Julia and me. You implied things."

"Did I?"

I glared at her.

"Let me ask you something," she said. "What do you think choice means in terms of everything we've been discussing here?"

"What do you mean?"

She clicked her pen. "You made choices. Presumably Julia did too, right?"

"Duh."

"Did she ever make ones that you didn't agree with? Or that hurt you?"

I looked down. My hands were knotted into fists on my lap. I forced them to relax. I stared at my fingers.

I thought about that time right after you got your car. The night we were supposed to go to Kenny Madden's party. I didn't want to go. I just wanted a break from it all, you know? Even when I drank I sometimes still felt too tall and stupid and too . . . me at parties.

You said, "Fine, it'll probably suck anyway," even though we both knew if you went you could hook up with a very hot senior who'd called earlier to make sure you were going. We stayed at your house and watched DVDs. You made fudge, and when your mother came home she didn't even bitch about the melted chocolate that had hardened on the counter, just laughed and said she'd clean it up in the morning. It was so much fun. I had so much fun.

I thought you did too.

But you didn't, I know you didn't, because after I fell asleep, you snuck out your window. You came back in the morning after your mom had already gotten up, walked in as I was trying to edge out your front door and away from your mom's furious face and accusations.

"Tell her I didn't do anything," I said to you. "Tell her I didn't even know you'd left."

"Where the hell were you?" your mother said. "Do you know how worried I was? Do you know how I felt when I looked in your room and you weren't there?"

"Whatever," you said, tossing your jacket on a chair and heading upstairs. "I'm so sick of you not wanting me to have any fun."

I never knew which one of us you were talking to.

I sat in silence till Laurie told me I could go.

NINETEEN

CARO CALLED the day after we went to the university library. I wondered why until I picked up the phone and she said, "Have you done the research you said you would yet?"

"I'm working on it," I said, and watched Mom, who'd answered the phone, wave at me and mouth, "I'll give you some privacy," before leaving the room, a huge smile on her face.

"Okay, good," Caro said. "It's just that you left kind of early, and Patrick basically bolted the second Mel and I came back again, so I was thinking that maybe you hadn't . . ." She trailed off. I stared at the ceiling and told myself I wasn't thinking about what Patrick had said to me.

"I guess I'd better go," she finally said, and we hung up. Mom came in a few minutes later, still smiling. I said, "It was just someone about an English project," before she could say anything, and then went back to doing my homework.

I could feel Mom watching me for a while, but she didn't say anything.

Caro called again, and it was a repeat of before with Mom's reaction, but after a few more calls—all the same, all about the presentation—Mom seemed to realize that my social life wasn't about to change. I thought I'd be glad that Mom stopped looking so hopeful every time she called me to the phone, but I sort of missed her smiling like she knew something good was going to happen and that she wanted it for me.

Then Caro called last night, completely frantic about our presentation.

"Hi," she said, when I picked up the phone. "Do you have any ideas about the role of the Mississippi in *Huck Finn*?"

"Well, since it was only all we talked about in class today, nope."

"Oh crap, it was all we talked about today. I'm an obsessive freak, aren't I?" she said, and laughed.

The laugh surprised me. I spent my days surrounded by people who were completely unable to relax about anything even remotely school related, but Caro—at least Caro could laugh about it.

"Nah. A real obsessive wouldn't have bothered saying hi first," I said.

She laughed again. "Hey, I—I have to go to Miller-town tomorrow afternoon to pick up something for my dad. Mom won't let me drive to school, so I have to go home and get the car before I can go. It's such a pain. Do you maybe want to meet me at my house and come with?"

"What?"

"Never mind," she said hastily. "I was just—it was a stupid idea. I've got a lot of homework so—"

"I'll go." I don't know why I said it, but I did.

Mom and Dad were so happy when I told them I was doing something with someone after school that I was afraid they might explode.

Then Dad said, "Who's Caro again?"

"I'm doing this thing, this presentation in English, with her," I said. "And you guys know her. She used to come over all the time when I was little."

"Oh, Caro," Mom said, and Dad nodded, but I knew neither of them remembered her.

"Well, that's great," Dad said. "I guess you won't need me to pick you up tomorrow."

"No, I will. You have to drive me to her house because Caro can't let anyone see me and her hanging out at school."

"I'm sure that's not the case," Dad said in a too-hearty voice that made even him look like he wanted to wince.

"Your father can drop you off," Mom said, and then changed the subject to the latest company Dad was trying to work with, putting her hand on top of his. I figured that meant all the phone calls that hadn't led to a glittering social life let her see this wasn't a big deal.

As usual, I was wrong.

When I got home tonight, Mom was waiting for me, and as soon as I came in she said, "So, how was it? Did you have fun?"

I shrugged.

"What did you do?"

I looked at her. "We drove to Millertown. We picked up a bowling trophy for her dad, and then we got cheese fries. Then she drove me home, and here I am. Now I'm going to go work on the presentation we have to do tomorrow."

I walked off before she could say anything else. I didn't want to talk about the afternoon with her. I just—I don't know.

It was fun. I had fun. The trophy me and Caro picked up—it was unbelievable. It was almost as tall as I am, and on top there was a guy standing with his arms in a victory V, one hand holding a bowling ball. We started laughing as soon as we saw it, and when we were eating our fries, she said, "Mom's already made my dad swear to keep it in the basement," and then imitated them arguing about it. I laughed so hard my sides hurt.

We didn't talk about school, we didn't even talk about Beth or Mel. We just . . . we just got a stupid trophy and ate fries, nothing really, but the whole time I didn't feel as bad as I usually do. I didn't hate myself so much.

Mom didn't quit, though. She came up to my room a few minutes later and said, "Well, I think it's great you went out. And you know what? I was thinking that this weekend we could go to Oasis and get our hair cut. Maybe we could even go to their spa, make a day of it."

"I'm growing my hair out." Julia always cut my hair. She was really good at it, and I know she would have had her own salon by the time she was twenty, just like she always said, and it would have been way better than Oasis. (Even if I never have been there.)

"Oh. Well, maybe we could go to the mall or something instead."

"I don't think I can. And look, I have a lot of homework, and the presentation is tomorrow, like I said, and I ate already, so I—you know. I need to focus."

Mom didn't do anything for a moment, and then she nodded and left.

I thought maybe Mom would come back and ask me to do something with her again, but she didn't. I went downstairs later to get a soda, and she and Dad were sitting at the kitchen table, holding hands and talking. They didn't even look up when I came in. They didn't seem to notice me at all. Totally familiar territory, and exactly what I wanted. It just didn't feel as great as I wanted it to.

I know things will go back to normal after tomorrow. Caro won't talk to me after the presentation, and it looks like things are getting back to how they were with Mom and Dad. It's good. It's all really good. It'll all be like it was. Like I deserve.

But then why . . .

Why do I feel so bad?

TWENTY

MEL AND CARO ended up doing all of the talking during our presentation, which was fine with me. I hadn't thought about what a class presentation really meant. How it was a whole standing-in-front-of-an-entire-room-of-people (annoying people, but still) thing. It was like being at a party, only worse because it was school, I wasn't drunk, and Julia wasn't there.

If there was a way I could have bolted out of class and gone and gotten a drink, I would have.

I suppose I could have. I could have walked out of class, out of school, and found a drink. But I didn't. Of course I didn't. I was too scared to move. I stood there, too tall, too quiet, tugging at the ends of my too-red hair, and missed J so much it felt like I couldn't breathe.

If Julia had been there, I could have gotten through today okay. Safely.

We were the last group to go, and when the bell rang Mel was still talking. Gladwell said, "Thank you all for a wonderful presentation," raising an eyebrow at me because I hadn't said a word the whole time. (But she didn't give Patrick the eyebrow. Apparently clicking a mouse counts as talking.)

Everyone left except us and the other two groups that had spoken. Of course they got their grades first. Caro disappeared into the hall before we got ours, though, because Beth gave her a look, and so me and Patrick and Mel were left standing there.

"You know," Mel said, "I thought about you when I was talking about Huck and Jim's friendship."

I (stupidly) nodded, figuring Mel was about to head off into one of his tangents where he asked me if I liked tacos or something, but instead he said, "You must really miss Julia. I mean, you never talk about her or anything, which is kind of weird, but I can just tell you do. I talked to her at parties a couple of times, you know. She had a great laugh. I remember this one time—" He kept talking and I thought about taking my copy of *Huckleberry Finn* and stuffing it in his mouth so he'd shut up.

I could actually see myself doing it. I wanted to do it.

I wanted to do it so badly it scared me.

Patrick cleared his throat. I looked at him, surprised. He looked away, of course. Mel glanced at him too but kept talking to me. "Anyway, what I'm trying to say is that I don't think Julia would have wanted you to be so sad."

I forced myself to nod. A few conversations at a party and Mel was qualified to tell me what Julia wanted? It was like being in freaking Pinewood or talking to stupid Laurie, where everyone was so sure they knew J and what she thought about her life and me even though they'd never met her.

"See, the thing about grief is—" Mel said, and Patrick shifted the laptop he was carrying, his elbow clipping Mel's side.

"Sorry," Patrick said. "Hey, can you go grab the CDs? I left them on the bookshelf in the back. I would get them, but I have to put all this stuff away before my next class."

"Sure," Mel said and patted my arm before he turned away.

"Thanks," I told Patrick, and I meant it. I thought he understood, and it was nice that someone knew that people telling you what you should feel sucks.

"Sure. The anger will go away, you know. Mostly, anyway."

"What?" That wasn't understanding at all, and I felt so stupid for thinking, even for a second, that someone could really get how I felt. It pissed me off.

He took a step back. "Never mind."

"No, go on. You were going to, what? Tell me I'm not sad, I'm angry at myself? Wow, you're a genius. Congratulations on observing the obvious!"

"You know what I mean," Patrick muttered.

"Whatever." I started to walk away. Hearing my grade could wait. I just wanted to get out of there.

"You're angry at her," he said. "At Julia."

I kept walking like I didn't hear him. But I did.

I should have just left it at that, but I had to sit through lunch and the rest of my classes, and even though I ignored Patrick I knew he was there. I saw him sitting in physics with both hands clamped to his lab table like they were bolted to it. He got up and left when we still had twenty minutes to go, saying he had to use the bathroom and never coming back.

And did anything happen to him? Did the teacher realize he was gone and report him? Of course not.

I got mad then. I got really mad. It was okay for him to leave class early, because he was smart and not a freak like me? It was okay for him to skulk around hallways and not talk during class presentations? But me not wanting to talk about Julia with the losers I'm stuck seeing in class?

Well, something must be wrong with me, and I shouldn't be so sad. But wait! I'm not sad, I'm mad at Julia!

I raised my hand and asked to go to the nurse's office. I told the nurse I had cramps. She let me lie down and went off to gossip with the secretaries. I used her phone to call Dad. He was on a conference call, but his secretary put me through.

I told him he didn't need to pick me up. I said I was going to the library. I said I was going with Caro. I said she was going to give me a ride home. He said, "That's wonderful, sweetheart," and sounded so happy. The "sweetheart" didn't even sound forced.

I should have called him back and said I'd changed my mind or something. Should have, should have, should have. Instead I flipped through the school directory in the nurse's desk and wrote down an address. Patrick lives in Meadow Hills, over by the golf course.

I took the bus there. His house looked like every other one on the street, white with big columns and a stained glass window over the front door. A woman shouted, "Come in!" when I knocked.

I didn't see anyone when I walked inside, but there was a television on in the room right in front of me, and past that I could see a kitchen with the fake marble linoleum Julia's mom always wanted. (And Julia was right, it looks horrible.)

There was a staircase just to my right, one of those split ones for people with houses on three levels. The upstairs part was barricaded with the gates people get for little kids. The downstairs part led to a hallway.

"I thought you weren't coming till after six!" It was the woman again, still shouting, and before I could say anything, she added, "I've got Milton in the tub, Wendy, so just go downstairs and get Patrick to help you carry the bikes out. He came home early to get them ready."

I went downstairs. I didn't bother knocking before I started opening doors. The first one led to a laundry room, and the second room was full of hospital-type stuff: a bed with railings, a wheelchair, and one of those walkers medical shows use during the very special episode when someone learns to walk again.

The third one was Patrick's room and Patrick was sitting on his bed, which was just a mattress on the floor. His room was a total mess, clothes and books and CDs everywhere, and I could barely get the door open. When

I did I just stood there, staring at him sitting cross-legged and hunched over his laptop.

He didn't even look up, and after a minute he said, "I know, I promised I'd get the bikes together and help with Dad before Wendy comes over, but I had a really bad day." I thought of a million things to say like, "Yeah, must be tough to get to leave class whenever you feel like it," or "I just came by to say you're a loser freak. Later," but instead I just stood there, and eventually he looked up and said, "Amy?" and I said, "You don't know how I feel."

I said that, and he looked at me for a long, silent moment, and then said, "You hate yourself," quietly, so quietly, and I clapped my hands together slowly, applause for a moron because of course I do, it's the most obvious thing in the world, and felt a smile cross my face because I'd shut him up.

Except I didn't because he said, "You hate her."

I stopped clapping and moved toward him like Julia used to when she was going to fight, deliberate steps, and for once being so tall was great because I'd be able to see the look in his eyes when I hurt him.

I wanted to hurt him. I wanted his words gone, shoved back down his throat, undone, unsaid. My mouth was open, my hands were curled, but I—

I didn't hit him. I could see it, my fists smashing into his face, his mouth opening not around words but breath, blood, but I didn't do it.

I didn't hit him. I remember seeing my hands, balled into fists and outstretched. I remember feeling something ripping up my throat, and then there was the bright whiteness of my knuckles smacking his chest. And my open mouth, the one that was so full of words ready to rip out of me, *you're so wrong so full of shit you hide from the world so what do you know?* It didn't form words.

I didn't say anything. I was silenced, like something inside me was broken. I just stood there, mouth open in a silent scream.

If he'd put his hands over mine, trying to comfort, I would have hit him. If he'd said something—anything—I would have hit him. If he'd done any of that, it would have been—I could have dealt with it. My hands have been touched earnestly a thousand times, by my parents, by stupid counselors at Pinewood who "just wanted to reach" me.

He just looked at me.

He looked at me, and I saw he didn't want me there, that having me in his home, in his room, in his space, was bothering him. He looked at me, and I saw that he wanted me to go so badly he couldn't say it, that he was afraid. That he knew what it was like to wake up every day and know that this life, the one you live, is not the one you ever saw or wanted but is yours all the same.

I always wanted to be grown up. When I was little I couldn't wait to be a teenager and go to high school. When I got there I wanted to be done with it, wanted to get out into the world, the real one, and live in it.

The thing is, that world doesn't exist. All growing up means is that you realize no one will come along to fix things. No one will come along to save you.

I put one hand on his throat. Palm down, resting against skin. He breathed, and I felt the rise and fall of his breath against my hand. I pressed my fingers in a little, flexing. Skin is so fragile.

The whole body . . . it shouldn't be like it is. It shouldn't be so easy to break. But it is, and in his eyes I saw he understood that too. I slid my hand up, rested it against his mouth, and in a moment replaced it with my own.

As soon as I did, I knew what would happen. It started one night, back when Julia was still here, and I pretended it away. It never happened, I told myself, but it did.

I touched my mouth to his because he hadn't done what I expected, hadn't tried to comfort me. I touched my mouth to his because he didn't say he was sorry for me, for my loss, or for what he'd said. I touched my mouth to his because he understood everything.

I touched my mouth to his because I wanted to. I kissed him, and this time I didn't run away.

Patrick smells like fall leaves, the orange-brown ones that blow around your feet when you walk and swing into your face smelling of sunshine and earth. His skin is cool and pale, and I've traced his back, mapping the play of muscles under skin. I've felt his mouth against mine. I've felt his hands on my skin. There is a scar on his stomach, round and white, tucked up against the side of one rib. It is smooth to the touch.

I know all these things, and now they will not leave me.

I lay there afterward, eyes closed, feeling his mouth ghost across mine, and felt . . . I don't know. I just know I felt okay.

I felt okay, and that wasn't how I was supposed to feel. I got up, tucked my body back into my clothes, and shook my head so my hair slid over and around my face, covering me. It's long now, almost to my shoulders. It hasn't been cut since before Julia died.

Patrick was dressed when I finally looked over at him, his head emerging from his T-shirt and a red flush along his cheekbones. He saw me looking and the red deepened, blossomed across his face. I opened my mouth, then closed it. He did the same.

I left his room, shut his door behind me. I didn't look back, not once, but I walked home feeling strange, like I'd somehow lost part of myself, like somehow part of me was still with him.

Was this how it was for Julia with Kevin? Did it feel like this? Did she see him when she closed her eyes? Did she see him even when he wasn't there? How could she stand it? Why would she want it?

I wish she was here. I wish. I wish. I wish.

I wish I didn't hate her so much for leaving me.

150 days

J—

I thought some stuff about you the other day, but I didn't mean it. I should have said so sooner, but it's just—after everything that happened with Patrick two days ago, I haven't been . . .

I wasn't myself then.

I wasn't.

Look, I know sex was a big deal to you, that you liked being with someone you thought you'd connected with, but I don't want that. I don't want a connection. It's a stupid word.

What does it mean, really? Connection.

Nothing. That's what it means, and I didn't connect with him. What happened didn't mean anything. It didn't, it doesn't, and I don't—I don't want to be thinking about it. About him. I don't want to wonder what he's thinking, what he's doing, if he's thinking of me—

God! Look what you've done to me. Look what you've made me into. I don't know why you—

We were both in your car. We both had our seat belts on. What was so different for you? That you were driving? You always drove. Why was that night so different? Why did you have to leave me?

Patrick was right, J. I hate myself.

But I hate you too.

152 days

J,

I meant what I said the other day. I hate you. I wish I didn't, but I do.

And knowing that—Julia, knowing that makes everything so much worse. I hate you for *dying*. It's beyond screwed up. If I was the one who'd died you'd miss me and maybe talk to that picture of us you kept tacked up on your dresser mirror, the one from Splash World, but you wouldn't write letters to me, boring wah-wah-wah letters.

You wouldn't blame me.

I miss you all the time; how you'd henna your hair because it was a Tuesday, the way you'd laugh and say, "A, you mope," when I said something stupid, how you somehow always knew when I needed a bag of salt-and-vinegar potato chips from the vending machine to get me through the last few periods of school, but the past couple of days I've missed you so much it's felt like missing you is all I am.

Like if someone looked inside me, there wouldn't be a skeleton and muscles and blood and nerves. There'd just be memories of you and all the things I've tried to say and ripped out of this notebook, all the things I want to say but can't because I don't have the words. You don't know how bad that makes me feel. How can you? I can't even begin to say.

I don't know what to do about Patrick. It's been four days, J. I haven't spoken to him since that afternoon. He hasn't spoken to me either. I should be happy about that.

I shouldn't be keeping track of how many days it's been. I shouldn't care if he ever speaks to me again or not. It was just sex, and I shouldn't even be writing about him. But I—

I keep thinking about him. His skin. His voice. The way—listen to me! It's like I'm in some freaking romance novel. It. Was. Just. Sex. What is wrong with me?

I have spoken to Mel. It was just once, two days afterward. The last time I wrote to you.

He came up to me after English and said, "You know why I asked you all those questions, right? And why

I brought Patrick to the movies?" an odd note in his voice.

"What?" I said, and looked around for Patrick before I could stop myself. He wasn't with Mel. In class, he'd sat at his desk (all the way across the room, now that our group project is over) staring at the door. He never looked at me, not once.

"Patrick," Mel said. "He's my friend, he likes you, and I thought that if I talked to you, asked all the questions I knew he wanted to, that maybe he'd get to the point where he'd talk to you himself. But—look, I don't know what happened, but I saw you two talking after our pre-sentation, and whatever you said to him, you need to do something about it, take it back or whatever, because he's acting really strange now."

I walked away. What else could I do? What could I say? "Well, actually, Mel, I did more than talk to him. We had sex. And I can't really take that back, can I?"

This is insanity. A couple of minutes of someone grunt-ing over you is just that and nothing more. You thought you were supposed to have feelings about it, about the guy. You couldn't see sex for what it is, a random moment with someone, a moment that has meaning only if you let it.

I can't believe that's what I used to say to you. That I said it whenever you were upset about a guy. I said it a lot to you about Kevin, didn't I? "This is insanity," and "it has meaning only if you let it." No wonder you always rolled your eyes and said I didn't understand.

I thought I did, but I didn't. I so didn't. Even though Kevin was a total ass because he cheated on you and lied about it (badly), he still meant something to you. When you were with him, it was always more than a random moment to you, and meaning wasn't something you could put there if you wanted to. It was just there, and you felt it.

I wish I'd gotten that before now. You don't know how much I wish it.

TWENTY-ONE

THIS AFTERNOON I went to Caro's after school, and her sister came over to show her a picture of the bridesmaid dresses. They were hideous, a weird orange-pink with ruffles everywhere. Plus there were matching hats.

I bit my lip so I wouldn't laugh, and Caro said, "Please tell me the hat has ruffles on it too, Jane. I don't think I can be in your wedding looking like a diseased piece of citrus fruit if I don't have a hat with ruffles to wear."

"I like the hats," Jane said. "And no, they don't have ruffles. Yet." She smiled at me, and then said, "And Caro, I love your hair," as she left.

"See?" I said, and Caro rolled her eyes at me, but she was smiling too. The other day I'd dragged her to the

237

drugstore to get some temporary hair color because she'd mentioned it like eight hundred times.

It turned out pretty good—I made her get purple—and this morning I heard Beth telling her how great it looked in the bathroom. Of course, it was a Beth compliment because she said, "Caro, your hair actually looks really nice for once!" Caro just smiled, but as they were walking out, she glanced at me and whispered, "Is it wrong that I want to jam a fork in her face?"

When we were waiting for the hair dye to process, I told Caro what Patrick had told me in the library, about Beth and the things she'd said to Mel. I thought she'd be surprised but she wasn't. She just sighed and said, "I know."

"You know?"

"Well, not exactly know, but it figures," Caro said. "See, back in September, right after school started, I got really drunk at a party and ran into Mel. We went outside and were standing around, just the two of us, and he looked so good that before I knew it, I told him I liked him. Then I ran off and threw up. I thought—he was drunk too, so I figured he didn't remember. I mean, he never said anything. But I was still so embarrassed I couldn't even look at him until we ended up in that group in English. And then it was like . . . I don't know. The way he talked to me, I thought maybe he liked me too. But then Beth said she liked him, and—"

"And that meant you couldn't."

"Yeah," Caro said. "But . . . okay. If I tell you something, will you be honest with me? I mean, will you tell me what you really think?"

"Yes. Beth's a complete shit."

She laughed. "Besides that. Remember when Beth told me to ask Mel if Joe was going to a party, and I told Mel I thought Joe was hot and acted like I—?"

"Wanted to hook up with him?"

Caro nodded. "Right. Beth did all that for a reason."

"Because she wanted Mel to think you liked Joe instead of him."

"Yeah, but here's the thing. I never told Beth what happened with Mel. I didn't tell anyone because it was so humiliating. So Beth never knew I liked Mel, which means—"

"Crap," I said. "It means Mel remembers what happened at the party—and told Beth about it. Why would he do that?"

"I don't know. But I guess when he and I talked in English and stuff, it was just talking. I guess he's always liked Beth."

I shook my head. "I don't think so. That one time he asked me to go to the movies with him, I could tell he liked you."

"Well, it doesn't really matter now," she said. "And, okay, what exactly was that movie thing about? Not that you aren't—I mean, it was just—"

"Very random?"

"Yeah."

I shrugged. I knew why Mel had asked me to the movies. He'd done it for Patrick, just like he'd asked me all those questions. No wonder he'd never looked interested in my answers. "I think your hair's done."

Caro looked at me, and for a second I thought she was going to say something. That maybe she had an idea of what had happened with me and Patrick. But she didn't say anything, and we just rinsed her hair out.

"It looks good," I told her when it was done.

"Thanks," she said, and I made a face at her.

"No, for real," she said. "Thank you."

I knew what she meant. She was thanking me for being there, for listening.

"It's not a big deal," I said, but it kind of was to me. For me. No one has said thank you to me for real in a long, long time.

152 days

J—

There's some other stuff I need to tell you, okay?

Caro and I are still talking. I've even gone to her house a couple of times. Don't get me wrong—it's not like I tell her stuff or anything like that. I know she's Corn Syrup, who trails Beth around school like a whipped loser. But she makes fun of herself for it, and . . . I don't know. She's not that bad.

God, this—just doing this, just writing to you—it's hard. I've never been nervous talking to you before, but I am now. I've wanted to tell you everything, but I would look at this notebook and think of what I said to you before and hate myself.

Talking to you used to be so easy and now . . . now I don't know. I don't know anything.

I wish I wasn't so angry. I wish I was a stronger person, a better one.

Mom and I talked the day after . . . after Patrick. She picked me up from school and drove me home. She followed me into the study when I went in there to do my homework and started talking. She said she was sorry she'd pushed me to go to the mall, that if she'd hurt me by talking about getting a haircut she didn't mean it.

You should have heard her, J. I always wanted her to sound the way she did then. I wanted that pleading note in her voice. I always wanted her and Dad to feel the way I did around them. I wanted them to realize that you can be in a room with someone and yet not really be there to them.

And yeah, it felt okay. But it didn't feel great. I sat there, watching her talk and trying so hard, and I—I felt sorry for her. For Dad. Things had changed so much for them so fast, and here she was stuck at home with me in the middle of the afternoon. She wasn't working on a paper or going over stuff for a class or talking to Dad or doing the things that used to make her glow.

She and Dad might not have noticed me before, but hell, at least they were happy.

"I'm sorry," I told her. "I'm—this really sucks."

"Amy," she said, her face crumpling. "Please don't say that. Your father and I are trying so hard, and if you would just let us—"

"No, I mean, I'm sorry for you. It sucks that you have to do all this. It must be really hard."

She started to cry. Like, really cry. She just stood there, face in her hands, her whole body shaking.

"This is never what I wanted for you," she said after a while, the words muffled by her fingers. I wanted to hug her, but I was afraid to. What do I know about comfort, about making things better? I only know how to make them worse.

TWENTY-TWO

158 DAYS, and I saw Laurie this afternoon.

For once, I'd actually been looking forward to seeing her. I figured if anyone would be willing to point out how horrible I am for what I've been thinking about J, it's her.

"I'm mad at Julia," I said as soon as I walked in, and waited for the pen clicking to start.

When it didn't, I sat down and added, "I'm mad at her for dying. I'm mad at her for listening to me that night. I . . . sometimes I hate her."

Laurie nodded. That was it. She *nodded*.

I stared at her. She stared back at me.

"Did you hear me?" I said. "My best friend died because of me, and sometimes I hate her."

"Why do you hate her? For dying? Or because she listened to you?"

"Both!" I said, almost shouting. "I made sure she saw her boyfriend cheating on her. Made sure she saw it, and didn't just hear about it. Then I told her we should go because she . . . she didn't tell him to go to hell like I thought she finally would. She didn't . . . she was so sad, and I did that. I broke her heart."

"Amy—"

"There's more," I said. "You know it. I know it. I told her to get in the car. I told her to drive. She did all that, she listened to me, and I hate her for that. She died and I hate her for that too. What's wrong with me?"

Laurie sighed. "Did Julia always do what people told her to?"

"You didn't listen to anything I said about her at all, did you? She always did her own thing. But that—" I broke off and glared at Laurie, because I knew what she was doing and I was sick of it, sick of her. "I know what you're going to say, I know what you're thinking, but it doesn't—it doesn't mean what you think it does. Julia didn't choose to die." My voice was shaking. My whole body was shaking.

"No, she didn't. But she chose to get into her car and drive, just like you chose to drink."

"That's it?" I said, and I was yelling now, full of fury and something else, something I didn't want to think about. "Just like that, just that simple, you say she chose to get into the car and I'm supposed to . . . what? Forget what I did? Say 'I see it now, I do, and yay! Laurie's made everything's okay!' and move on?"

"If you can see your choices, why can't you see hers?"

"Because it's not that simple. Because you can't—you can't make everything all right," I said, and stood up. I walked out of her office, and I slammed the door behind me so hard it shook. I wished it would crack in half. I wished Laurie's office would crumble around her.

To my surprise, she came right out after me.

"No one ever said what happened was simple," she said, her voice firm. She motioned for me to come back inside.

"Why?" I said. "So you can tell me more about choices?"

"Because you're right," she said. "I can't make everything okay for you."

I hadn't expected that, so I went back in and sat down.

She followed me, and as soon as she was in her chair, she picked up her pen. I knew it was coming at some point, but now? I glared at her and started to stand up again, but then stopped, frozen. Frozen because I knew what I'd felt right before I left. I was angry, so angry, but I also wanted—I wanted to believe her too. But like she said, she couldn't make everything okay.

"You know what?" I said, staring at that stupid pen and hating myself for wanting to believe her. For wanting to think I didn't kill Julia. "Here's something new for you. I had sex with someone. Why don't you tell me how I should feel about that?"

Laurie just looked at me.

"Go on," I said, my voice rising again, and she said, "How do you want to feel about it?"

"I don't feel anything," I said, but my voice cracked a little. "It was just—it was the first time I did it when I wasn't drunk and it was . . . it was different. That's all."

Laurie uncrossed and recrossed her legs. "Different how?"

"I don't know. Just different."

"I see." Laurie clicked her pen, finally. And when she did, when I heard that click, something clicked in me, and I got why she did it. Why I'd heard all that pen clicking time after time after time.

Laurie clicks her pen when she thinks I'm lying to her. When she thinks I'm lying to myself.

"It was different—it was different because I liked it," I said after a moment, my voice quiet. Saying what I knew but hadn't been able to let myself say before. Hadn't even been able to let myself see before. "I liked being with him. I never cared about being with guys before. But with him it was—it meant something to me, and I . . . I don't know."

I waited for her to say something. Anything. I'd told her everything, I'd told her the truth I hadn't wanted to see.

She just looked at me.

"Aren't you going to say something?" I finally asked.

"What do you want me to say?"

"I don't know."

"I can't make everything okay for you, Amy. You said it yourself. But I can tell you this. What you told me just now isn't about Julia. It's about you. And you have to make choices of your own, choices only you can make, so I'm going to ask you something, and I want you to answer honestly. Can you do that?"

"No."

For a second, I swear she almost smiled. "Do you want to be happy?"

"Yes. No. I don't know. What kind of question is that?"

"A simple one," she said. "Do you want to be happy?"

"I don't—I don't think I know how."

"So you can learn," she said.

TWENTY-THREE

DURING DINNER TONIGHT, Mom and Dad asked me to watch a movie with them. I took a bite of black bean burrito and chewed for as long as I could, hoping they'd ask me something else, or at least stop looking at me. I was still processing the Laurie thing from yesterday, was still raw from the things she said, the things I'd felt, and wasn't ready to do anything else, much less play happy family.

"You can decide which one while your father clears the table," Mom said, and grinned at Dad before looking at me. I stared down at my plate. I didn't want to see her grin falter. I wish I'd never seen her cry like I did the other day because no one's life should be driving their kid home from school and then sobbing.

"Oh, I see how it is," Dad said. "You want me out of the way to influence the selection. You're sneaky and beautiful."

Mom laughed and I watched the two of them sparkle and wondered why we kept pretending. I was so tired of them trying to be what they'd never wanted to be before, of the whole "we're available! and dedicated!" parents routine. I was tired of how they were always acting like they didn't mind living with me.

"You know you love my taste in movies," Dad said, picking up his plate and Mom's and kissing the top of her head. She tilted her head back and grinned at him.

I never thought my parents deserved their . . . thing, their endless swallow-up-everything love. I hated it because it made me nothing. Love, to me, was all about exclusion.

I hated that we weren't a family. We were a couple with an extra person tacked on because they simply happened to forget birth control one night sixteen years ago. They've never said it—not directly to me, anyway—but I heard them talking about it once. Mom realized she was going to have me, and eight months before I was born, Dad had a vasectomy. You don't forget hearing something like that.

I pushed my plate away.

"You don't have to do this anymore," I said. "You don't have to play perfect family with me. Things can go back to how they were."

My father froze. So did my mother, head still tilted back toward him, the smile on her face fading.

"All right, I promise I won't suggest any possible movies," Dad said, trying for normal but failing. Teenagers only want to spend evenings bonding with their parents in old sitcoms, and no one in this house ever asked me to watch a movie with them before Julia died. And no matter what Laurie had said and how much part of me wanted to believe her, believe that I'd made choices and Julia had made them too, I couldn't—I couldn't forget what I'd done.

"Look," I said, and my voice was rising, all the things I'd wanted to say and never had spilling out. "I know your story, yours and Mom's. True love forever and ever, and then I came along and made the perfect couple into perfection plus an eight-pound shackle. You don't have to pretend that this"—I gestured at the three of us—"is what you want."

Dad sat down, the plates he was carrying making a cracking noise as they hit the table. He looked at me like he'd seen something surprising. Maybe even frightening. Even when he came into the emergency room the night Julia died he hadn't looked at me like that.

"It's true," he said after a moment, his voice very quiet. "Your mother and I love each other very much. And it's true that we—that we didn't plan on having children. But Amy, it doesn't mean we didn't want you. That we don't love you very much and want to make things better for—"

"Stop," I said, and looked at Mom. "Please, just stop this. Make Dad stop. Make all of it stop. I saw you the other day. I was there. I made you cry. I know you can't stand this. That you can't stand what I did."

"Amy, that's not—that's not why I cried." She stretched her hands across the table toward me. "I cried because I can't reach you. I can't stand to see you so sad, so determined to be alone. Your father and I, we need to be better parents to you, need to—"

I shoved her hands away. "Why are you doing this? Why are you pretending? You know what I did to Julia. You know I—"

"Don't," Mom said, her voice shaking, and I could see the words she didn't want to hear written on her face.

"I killed her. You know that. I know that. Why can't you just—why won't you just say it?"

"Because you didn't!" Dad said, pushing away from the table and running a hand through his hair. "How can you even say it? How can you even think it?"

"How can I not?" I said. "I told her to get in the car!"

"But she chose to do it," Mom said.

I shook my head, shoving her words away, shoving away her echo of what Laurie had said. Shoving away how those words—from Laurie, and now from Mom—made me think, hope.

Mom leaned over and grabbed my hands.

"Listen to me," she said, and when I tried to pull away, she wouldn't let go. She held on to me. "We all make choices, Amy. Sometimes we make good ones. Sometimes we make bad ones. You made choices that night, but Julia made them too. What happened was terrible, but it isn't your fault—it isn't—and you have to stop blaming yourself."

"I—but if I didn't do it, then it—"

"It was an accident," Dad said, and his voice was so gentle. So sure. "A horrible one, one where you lost your best friend, but that's what it was. What it is."

"But—" My eyes were burning, all of me was burning, shaking, and Mom said, "Amy, honey, it's all right," and then she put her arms around me, she was hugging me.

She hugged me, and I let her. I wanted her to.

"Your father and I want to spend time with you, we want to be here for you," she said. "We want you to see that Julia's death isn't your fault. We want to be a family. Those are our choices."

"I —" I pulled away, and looked at her. I looked at her, and then at Dad.

"Try," Dad said. "Try to see how much we love you, try to see that Julia didn't die because of you. That's all we ask. Just . . . try. Please." He cleared his throat, blinking hard. "Now, do you know what movie you want to watch?"

So I picked a movie, and we watched it. I didn't know what else to do, and everything else, all the things they said, I . . .

I want to believe them.

I think about what Laurie said, about learning to be happy, and think that maybe—that maybe I can learn how to do that. How to be that.

Maybe.

Julia's still gone, though. I still have to live with that. I still have to live without her.

TWENTY-FOUR

I WENT TO A PARTY TONIGHT.

There's six words I never thought I'd say again.

The party was at Mel's. His parents are in Aruba or something. I wasn't invited, obviously—Mel hasn't spoken to me since he asked me what I'd done to Patrick—but I knew all about it because Mel talks very loudly and also because right after English today he asked Caro if she was going.

Actually, what he said was, "I really hope you can come tonight. I need to talk to you." And he said all that in front of Beth. I was in the student resource center during lunch, so I missed the drama, but Caro's eyes were red afterward so it was easy to guess what happened.

I was in the student resource center because I've given up on lunch in the cafeteria. It's not worth the daily race with mustache girl to get a crappy seat and eat crappy food. I can eat yogurt in the resource center instead. The whole thing was Giggles's idea, actually.

She cornered me as I was skulking down the hall, late to physics class, and made me come to her office. (Patrick had been standing outside the classroom door, looking like the world was going to come smash him in that way he does, and I'd ducked into the bathroom till after the bell rang. Fifteen days. It's been fifteen days, and I still keep thinking about him.)

When Giggles realized I didn't have enough tardies for detention, she said I needed to "give back to the school" and told me I had to work in the resource center every day during lunch for a month.

I can't wait to see the look on her face when I tell her I want to keep doing it. Maybe I'll even say she's inspired me. She'll probably explode.

Anyway, Caro came up to me in the hall after physics and said, "Can you come over after school?" while people—meaning Beth—were watching. That's when I knew something huge was going on.

Caro didn't want to go to the party. What Mel had said to her made Beth so furious that she'd stopped talking to Caro.

"Which explains why you actually spoke to me at school," I said as we were sitting in her bedroom. I was lying on her bed and Caro was pacing around eating an ice cream bar. Her mom always buys the kind I like best now. I didn't think I was over here that much, but I guess I am.

Caro looked at me and then tossed her wrapper in the trash. "Yeah, I guess it does. I sort of suck, don't I? Why do you even talk to me?"

"Free ice cream. And besides, if I were you, I wouldn't talk to me at all."

"You would too."

I rolled my eyes at her. "You're the worst liar in the whole world."

She flopped down on her bed and nudged me with one foot. "Fine. I'm too freaked out to argue with you. What am I going to do?"

"Go to the party and talk to Mel."

"But Beth will—"

"What? Make you cry during lunch? Get you so upset you ask someone even the honors losers—sorry, but it's true, you guys suck—avoid to come over after school in front of everyone?"

She sighed. "I know. But I can't go."

"Okay, don't go."

"But . . . I kind of want to go."

"Duh."

Then she surprised me. "So will you come with me?"

And that's how I ended up at the party. I told Mom and Dad I was spending the night at Caro's. I figured that and the fact that they hadn't had to come pick me up after school was enough excitement for them. Mentioning a party would just be too much.

And besides, I didn't think I'd actually go. I just . . . I couldn't see it. I couldn't see myself at one without Julia. I figured I'd wait outside or something. Be alone.

That, I could see.

Caro and I went over her "plan" on the way there. She was going to go in and talk to Mel, then leave. I was supposed to stay with her the whole time.

"Seriously, you can't leave my side," she said.

"Seriously, you've already said that. But you don't need me there."

"I do too."

"Fine," I said, just to humor her. "But remember, you promised that even if Mel declares eternal love we won't be there more than—"

"Ten minutes, tops. I know. We'll go in, he'll be with Beth, we'll leave. I don't even know why I'm doing this."

"Yeah, you do," I said, and tried not to think about the fact that I was going to a party and that the last one I went to was with Julia. It didn't work, and by the time Caro and I walked inside Mel's house, I was feeling really bad. Just walking through the door made me dizzy.

And inside, my stomach hurt, my hands were sweaty and shaking, and I could tell people knew I didn't belong.

I've always felt like that at parties. It's why I started drinking before J and I got there, so that walking inside wouldn't be so hard. I needed that escape from myself.

I turned to Caro, ready to tell her I needed to leave, that I had to leave, when Mel showed up. He looked as freaked as I felt and like he was trying to hide from someone.

"I'm so glad you're here," he told Caro, and that's when I knew Beth was out there, in the crowd of people around us, newly single and extremely unhappy about it. "Can we go somewhere and talk?"

Caro looked at me and I knew the ten-minute, we-stick-together plan was gone. I don't know why I even fell for it in the first place. How many times did I agree to it when Julia and I went to parties where Kevin was going to be and end up alone?

"I can't," she said. "Amy and I can only stay for a few minutes."

"Oh," Mel said, and looked at me. "I didn't know you were coming."

Classy. "Nice to see you too."

"That's not what I meant. Sorry." He ran a hand through his hair, looked out at everyone carefully pretending they weren't watching, and then looked back at Caro. "Just a few minutes. Please."

"Are you feeling okay? Do we need to go?"

I looked at Caro and realized she was talking to me. I realized she was going to tell Mel she couldn't talk and that we had to go. Not because she didn't want to talk to him, but because she'd realized I was freaked out and was willing to leave so I could get out of there.

I know she was terrified of running into Beth too. But she did mean it because when I said, "No, go talk to him," she shook her head and whispered, "I'm sorry. I should have realized—this must be so hard for you."

"Go," I said, and plastered what I hoped was a smile on my face.

"Ten minutes," Caro said, and then she and Mel disappeared into the crowd. I forced myself to look around even though my hands were shaking. Even though all of me was shaking.

This was what I saw:

People were dancing. People were making out. People were drinking. People were talking.

That was it. That's all there was to see.

Just people having fun, and I knew it was stupid to worry about being there. It was stupid to be scared.

But I was scared. I wanted to get out of there.

But more than that, I wanted a drink.

And since I was at a party, I knew I could get one. There was a keg and a bunch of bottles on a make-shift bar not too far away, in the corner of the room. Twenty steps, maybe. All I had to do was walk over there.

I couldn't.

I couldn't because if the people were less lame and the music was louder and the room a little darker, I could have been at the last party I went to. I could have been with Julia.

I walked away, tottering in my flat-soled sneakers like they were a pair of those monster shoes Julia would strap herself into, the ones with the stacked heels that made me so tall I smacked my head into her bedroom door the time she dared me to try them on.

I walked away, but I didn't leave. I wanted that drink, I wanted to forget, and I'd been to enough parties to know where to look for the parental liquor stash, for those bottles that had been hidden because they're the ones that are monitored.

Even wobbling and sweating, J's face at that last party all I could see, I found it in less than five minutes. Mel's parents had a very nice liquor cabinet, with a tricky lock, but when I got it open it was empty.

Mel might have been dating Beth, but he's still pretty smart.

I could have left then. Probably should have. But I knew where to look next, though, and headed upstairs, pretended not to see the bedrooms with their closed doors, pretended J's face wasn't all around me, and went straight for the bathroom.

I found the liquor cabinet stash and a set of monogrammed glasses in the bathroom hamper, under a pile of dirty and wet towels. There was scotch, bourbon, and a nice bottle of vodka, the kind that's good enough to come in glass, not plastic.

My hands were shaking when I opened the vodka, but not because I was scared. No, I wasn't scared anymore. I wanted a drink, I wanted that escape from my thoughts. From everything. God, I wanted it.

I poured myself a cup and then put the bottles back, my sweet little secret.

I was never labeled an alcoholic. Not even at Pinewood. Why? Because I didn't drink all the time. I drank too much, too often, but I didn't drink every day. I could stop, and had.

Binge drinking, I was told over and over again. It's dangerous, but common in teenagers, especially girls. What I did wasn't a sickness, wasn't a disease, and one day, when I was of legal age and much more sound mind, I would be able to drink normally. I think hearing that was supposed to make me feel better.

It's bullshit. It's so easy to label people, to look at a list of symptoms and say, "This is who you are. This is what you are." Everyone—teachers, J's mother, even people at school—they did that to Julia. She lived life fast and loud and fun. She didn't listen when people who were used to being listened to talked. She had sex. She took drugs. Sometimes she drank. Checklist marked, she was trouble.

Except she wasn't. She had a huge laugh, an even larger heart, and just needed to live in a world where it was okay to be under eighteen and have a mind of your own.

I will never be able to drink normally. I don't want to. When I think about drinking, it's release from myself I crave. I don't need to drink to get through the day, to smooth over problems, or because I want the drink itself.

I want to drink because I don't want to be who I am. My problem, my disease, is myself, and I stopped drinking because Julia was dead and I wanted to feel exactly who I am. I wanted to remember what I did.

I knew I should put the drink down. Thanks to Pinewood and Laurie, I knew I was supposed to stop and think about what led me here. That I needed to think about what trying to outrun myself gave me. What it had cost.

I knew I should put the drink down because of Julia. Because she was gone, and even if I hadn't made it happen, even if driving was her choice, I was still living with mine.

I didn't put it down. I drank. I didn't even notice the taste of the vodka. I didn't care about it. I never have.

I drank, feeling that familiar heat on my tongue, in my throat, warming my stomach, a sign that soon I'd stop feeling so small, so stupid, so me. I drank and then walked back toward the stairs, ready to face the party. I knew it wasn't a big deal. I knew it because I could walk back upstairs whenever I wanted and fill the glass I held over and over again.

Patrick was sitting at the top of the stairs. He was looking down at the party through the railing, watching everyone below us. I knew the look on his face. The "why" look: Why can't I have fun like they are? Why can't I just be normal? Why am I here?

When he turned and looked at me I froze. There he was, right in front of me, and everything—that night in the basement, all the things he'd said to me, that afternoon in his room—came rushing in all at once, filling my head.

I tightened my grip on the glass. I saw him see it. Saw him look at it, then me.

I was able to move then. I lifted the glass for another sip.

He didn't say anything. I didn't say anything. I drank.

He watched me. I closed my eyes so I didn't have to see him. When I opened them, my mouth and throat on fire, my closed eyes stinging, he spoke.

"Can I have some?"

I stared at him. Fifteen days and what he said, it wasn't—it wasn't what I expected him to say. But then, he never said what I thought he would.

The thing is, deep down in a part of me I wish I didn't have, a strange stupid soft spot full of hopes I try so hard to pretend away, I'd thought maybe he'd say something else. That maybe he could be someone to me. That I could be someone to him.

Deep down I thought I created the same spark in him that he did in me.

I held the glass out to him. He took it, careful not to let our hands touch. I wish I hadn't noticed that, but I did and it stung.

He closed his eyes when he drank too.

"God, that tastes like shit," he said when he was done. "Are you sure you want it back?"

I didn't say a word, just held out one hand for the glass. He didn't give it to me, but that was okay. I was going to take it and march back to the bathroom for a refill—no, the whole bottle. I was going to take it and then ignore Patrick like he was a bad dream, go down to the party and . . . nothing.

I didn't want to go to the party. There was nowhere I wanted to go. No one I wanted to see. My hands were shaking again.

"Give me the glass," I said.

He closed both hands around it. "Remember when I told you I once talked to Julia? I talked to her about you. It was last spring, the Monday after—after that party in Millertown. I went up to her right before third period. The halls were so crowded. I can still see it, all those people, but I went up to her and I told her—"

If I'd still been holding the glass, I would have dropped it then. He'd talked to Julia, and she'd never told me. I couldn't believe it.

"She never said anything. You told her about what we . . . you told her what happened?"

He shook his head. "I told her I'd talked to you at the party. That I . . . that I liked you. I thought maybe she'd help me talk to you. That night, you—you just disappeared. I even went into the party looking for you, but you were gone. When we . . . when we were in the basement, it was the only time in I don't know how long that I hadn't thought about how screwed up I am. But when I was done talking she—"

I could guess what happened then. Julia hated third period because she hated history, and anyone who tried to talk to her beforehand usually got their ass handed to them. I met her at her locker before and after every class except that one.

"She didn't say anything, just slammed her locker shut and walked off, right?"

"No," he said. "She said, 'She never said anything about you.' And then she looked at me. It was just for a second, but she had the strangest look on her face. Then she slammed her locker shut and walked away."

That's when I knew I was an even worse friend to Julia than I thought I was. That I'd let her down before I made sure she saw Kevin cheat, before I took her hand and led her to her car. When he mentioned the look on her face.

Julia had asked about Patrick. The Monday after that party, we were walking down the hall after fourth period and she said, "Hey, did you meet some guy at the party?"

I'd glanced over at her, and she was looking at me. I couldn't read the look on her face.

"No," I said, freaked out by how hard my heart had started pounding from just the mention of that party. That night. "At least, no one worth mentioning."

That look stayed on her face. I didn't get it, but I knew I wanted that guy and that night and the way I'd felt—so unsafe, so raw—gone, so I said something I knew would grab J's attention. "Hey, I think I see Kevin at the end of the hall."

It worked, but that strange look on Julia's face took a while to fade.

She was hurt. That's what that look was. I'd promised to always tell her everything, the kind of promise little kids make and forget, but she didn't. She needed it.

Julia needed to know there was one person who'd always listen to her. Who she could tell anything, and who'd tell her everything in return. I knew her so well. How could I not know what that look on her face meant?

Because I was afraid. Not of her, but of me. Of what I felt that night, of how for a moment I felt like myself in a way I hadn't ever before.

I swallowed, my eyes stinging.

"She did talk to me about it," I whispered. "She asked me about the party. About a guy. You. And I—I said there wasn't anyone worth mentioning."

"Oh," he said, and took another sip, eyes closing once more.

When he was done, he looked down at the party and then held the glass out toward me. "I figured that. I mean, I knew what happened didn't mean what I—I knew it wasn't a big deal. It's just that the other day, I thought that you—that we . . ." He shook his head. "Never mind."

I stared at the glass. I stared at him. I wanted the glass but I wanted to touch him too. I wanted to touch him so bad it hurt. I didn't want feelings like that. I'd never wanted them, but I hadn't known—I hadn't known how they really felt.

I'd never let myself know what it was like to want someone and know they want you too. It's a terrible feeling, makes you open yourself up, expose all the soft places you wish you didn't have.

It makes you hope.

"I lied," I said. "I lied to Julia. I didn't know what else to do because you—you make me feel . . ." I had to stop. Not because I didn't have words. I did. But I was afraid to say them.

He looked at me, and I knew then I could love him. That if I let myself, I would.

"You make me feel too," he said, and held out one hand. I looked at it. I looked at the glass in his other hand.

I reached out and closed my hand around the glass. It fit in my hand like it belonged there, and I knew if I drank from it I wouldn't have to say another word.

January 20th

Dear Julia,

I know it's been a while. I just . . . I had some things to work out. Things I had to do on my own. Things I had to do without you.

I put the glass down, J. I put it down and took Patrick's hand. Are you surprised? I was. I didn't think I could do things like that, take chances by myself, for myself. But I did. I did and I'm glad.

I don't know where we're going. Neither of us is very good at thinking about what might happen, about the "future." We just focus on now and it's enough, more than enough, because when he touches me I think of all those stupid love songs you used to sing and am glad I know the words. (Don't tell anyone I told you that.)

Your mother moved away about a month ago. She sold your house. No one knows where she went. She called my parents right before she left. She asked to speak to me.

She wanted to know what you said after the crash. She wanted to know your last words. She said I owed her that. She said I owed you that. She was crying.

You never said anything. You were already gone by the time I opened my eyes.

I told her you asked for her. That day in the cemetery, she said she'd give anything to hear your voice one last time, and I wanted her to have that. I wanted her to know you loved her. She was silent for a moment, and then she hung up. I don't know if she believed me or not.

Caro and I went to the mall today. We hang out a lot now. Mel asked her out the night of the party. He said he knew what Beth had told him was a lie, that he remembered the night Caro told him she liked him, and that he knew she meant it. He said he never meant to tell Beth about it, and was sorry he ever had. He said he wanted to be with her, not Beth.

She said no.

Beth found out everything, and didn't care that Caro said no. She trashed her and Mel all over school. A week after the party, when we were sitting together in the student resource center avoiding lunch, I asked her what she was going to do about Mel, who'd been calling her.

"Nothing," she said. "I liked him, and he knew it. He always knew it, he even said so—and he still chose to go out with Beth. He picked her, and even though he changed his mind, I want a guy who will pick me first. Mel can call all he wants, but I deserve better."

"You do," I told her, and I meant it. She's not you, J, but she's—she's becoming a friend.

At the mall we looked for a gift for Jane. The wedding is in about a month, on Valentine's Day. It's so cheesy it's sort of sweet. Caro says Jane's fiancé's cousin, who is in the wedding party, is flying in a few days early. He's in his freshman year at Cornell, but they met at a shower a few weeks ago and have been talking ever since. She says he's really nice.

I was asking her about him when we passed a girl with long, honey-colored hair. She was laughing loudly, freely. I stopped and stared. You know who I thought I saw. She smiled at me—it wasn't your smile—and then turned away.

I hated you for dying. For leaving. I hated you so much. I hated you almost as much as I hated myself. But I can look in the mirror now and face what I see. I'm even happy now, sometimes, and I can think of you and smile.

I won't lie and say everything's changed, though. I'm not a better person, a stronger one. I'm still me and I know what I did. Yeah, I wasn't driving the car, and I see the choices you made now. I even see that I can't make them mine, but I'll always remember making sure you saw Kevin.

I'll always remember taking your hand and telling you that everything would be okay.

Wherever I go, I'll always see you. You'll always be with me. And there's no happy ending coming here, no way a story that started on a night that's burned into my heart will end the way I wish it could. You're really gone, no last words, and no matter how many letters I write to you, you're never going to reply. You're never going to say good-bye.

So I will.

Good-bye, Julia. Thank you for being my friend. Thank you for being you.

Love,
Amy